THIS SERIES IS DEDICATED BY THE PUBLISHER TO THE MEMORY OF

JOHN CALDER AND MARION BOYARS

Mercury Books, an imprint of Michael Walmer, is set up to republish major works in translation which have been hard to procure in nice editions. The series design is an homage to the pioneering designs of the great John Sewell for Calder and Boyars.

MONEY and other stories

MERCURY BOOKS

MONEY
and other stories

by

KAREL ČAPEK

with a foreword by
John Galsworthy

translated by
Francis P. Marchant, Dora Round, F. P. Casey and O. Vočadlo

Mercury Books

ADELAIDE
MICHAEL WALMER
2019

Money and other stories (Trapné povídky) first published 1921

This translation first published 1930

This Mercury Books edition published 2019

by

Michael Walmer
9/2 Dahlmyra Avenue
Hamley Bridge
South Australia 5401

ISBN 978-0-6485905-0-7 paperback

ERRATA

This edition has been created utilizing a previous edition; thus errors have been reproduced. On page 29, line 30, for *again* please read *against*; on page 121, line 19, for *Work's* please read *Works*; on page 132, line 28, for *who do you* please read *why do you*; on page 182, line 5, for *Pauline* please read *Paulina*; and on page 187, line 27, also for *Pauline*, please also read *Paulina*.

ACKNOWLEDGMENT

Certain of these short stories have already appeared in *The London Mercury*, *The Fortnightly Review*, *The New Adelphi*, *The New Criterion*, *The London Aphrodite* and *Colour*.

FOREWORD

KAREL ČAPEK is best known to us English as the forceful and original author of *R.U.R.* and *The Insect Play* and for a diverting book of gently satirical impressions of English people and places. But, though young, he has already behind him a considerable body of work, and has earned an enviable reputation in Europe and America. He has a searching mind, a detached and lively fancy, and a real gift of expression. He is of the company that counts.

I have been asked to contribute a preface to this his first book of short stories in the English language. But good wine needs no bush, and good stories no preface; all I am going to say is that I read them with very lively interest—they are penetrating, they are unusual, they have power, and they have flavour.

JOHN GALSWORTHY.

Translated from the Czech
by
Francis P. Marchant, Dora Round,
F. P. Casey and O. Vočadlo

MONEY

Again, again it had come over him; he
had scarcely swallowed a few mouthfuls of food when a painful heaviness
seized him; a perspiration of faintness broke
out on his forehead. He left his dinner
untouched and leaned his head on his hand,
sullenly indifferent to the landlady's officious
solicitude. At length she went out sighing,
and he lay down on the sofa meaning to
rest, but in reality to listen with alarm and
attention to torturing sounds within him.
The faintness did not pass off; his stomach
seemed to have become a heavy stone, and
his heart throbbed with rapid, irregular beats:
from sheer exhaustion he perspired as he lay.
Ah, if he could only sleep!

After an hour the landlady knocked: she
handed him a telegram. He opened it in alarm
and read " 19.10. 7.34. Coming to-night.
Rosa." What this might mean he simply
could not grasp; bewildered, he stood up
and read through the numbers and words,
and at length understood: his married sister

Rosa would arrive this evening and, of course, he must go and meet her. Probably she was coming to do some shopping, and he felt annoyed at the hasty, feminine thoughtlessness and disregard for others, which disturbed him for no reason at all. He paced up and down the room, irritated because his evening was spoiled. He was thinking how comfortably he would have rested on his old sofa, soothed by the humming of his faithful lamp, with a book in his hand; he had passed weary and tedious hours there, but now for some unknown reason they seemed to him especially attractive, full of wise musings and very peaceful. A wasted evening, an end to rest. Full of childish and resentful bitterness, he tore the luckless telegram to fragments.

But that evening, when he was waiting in the lofty, cold, damp station for the belated train, a wider feeling of distress took possession of him : distress at the squalor and poverty around him, the weary folk who arrived, the disappointment of those who had been waiting in vain. With difficulty he found his fragile little slip of a sister in the thick of the hurrying crowd. Her eyes were frightened and she was dragging a heavy trunk along ; and at once he saw that something serious had happened. He put her into a cab and took her straight home. During the journey it occurred to him that he had neglected to find a room for her ; he asked her if she would like to go to an hotel, but this only evoked an outburst of tears. He really could do nothing with her in that state, so he gave it up, took her thin, nervous hand in his, and was immensely cheered when she at length looked up at him with a smile.

Once at home he looked closely at her and was alarmed. Distressed, trembling, strangely excited, with flaming eyes and parched lips, she sat there on his sofa, supported by the cushions which he heaped round her, and talked. . . . He asked her to speak softly, for it was already night. " I have run away from my husband," she burst out, talking quickly. " Ah, if you knew, George, if you knew what I have had to bear ! If you knew how hateful he is to me ! I have come to you to advise me," and then she burst into a flood of tears.

Gloomily George paced the room. One word after another called up before him a picture of her life with an overfed, money-grubbing, and vulgar husband, who insulted her before the servant, was ill-timed and immoderate in his affection, plagued her with endless scenes about nothing, foolishly squandered her dowry, was self-indulgent at home, and at the same time spent extravagantly on the silly whims of a hypochondriac. He heard the story of food doled out bite by bite, of reproaches, humiliations and cruelty, shabby generosity, frenzied and brutal quarrels, exacted love, stupid and overbearing taunts. . . . George paced the room choking with disgust and sympathy: it was intolerable, he could not endure this endless torrent of shame and pain. And there sat the small, fragile, capricious girl whom he had never thoroughly known, his proud and violent little sister; she had always been combative, and refused to listen to reason, her eyes used to flash wickedly when she was a small girl. There she sat, her chin quivering with sobs and with the ceaseless torrent of words, exhausted and feverish. George wanted to soothe her, but was half afraid. " Stop," he said roughly, " that will do, I know all about it." But he was powerless to restrain her.

" Don't," wept Rosa, " I have no one but you." Then the stream of complaints began again, more broken, at greater length, in calmer tones: details were repeated and incidents enlarged upon. Suddenly Rosa stopped and asked:

" And you, George, how are you getting on ? "

" As for me," grumbled George, " I can't complain. But tell me, won't you go back to him ? "

"Never," declared Rosa excitedly. "That is impossible. I'd rather die than . . . If you only knew what it was like!"

"Yes, but wait," observed George. "In that case, what do you think of doing?"

Rosa expected that question. "I made up up my mind about that a long time ago," she said warmly. "I will give lessons or go somewhere as a governess, to an office or anywhere. . . . You will see how I can work. I will get my living all by myself, and be so happy, so happy doing anything. You must advise me. . . . I will find a room somewhere, just a little one. . . . Tell me, something will turn up, won't it?" She could not sit still for excitement, but jumped up and, with an eager face, paced the room beside her brother: "I have thought it all out. I will take the furniture, the old furniture you know, which belonged to our parents; wait till you see. I really want nothing, but to be left in peace. I don't mind if I am poor, if only I don't have to . . . I want nothing else, nothing more in life than that, so little will suffice! I shall be satisfied with anything only if I am right away from— from all that. I am looking forward to working, I will do all my own sewing and sing over it—I have not sung for years. Ah, George, if you only knew!"

"Work," reflected George doubtfully. "I

don't know if any can be found—and anyway, you are **not** accustomed to that, Rosy, it will be hard for you, very hard."

" No," retorted Rosa with flashing eyes. " You don't know what it has been to be reproached for every mouthful, every rag, for everything. . . . All the time to be told that you don't work but only spend. . . . I should like to tear off all these things, it's all become so hateful to me. No, Georgie, you will see how glad I shall be to work, how happily I shall live. I shall enjoy every mouthful, even if it is only dry bread : I shall be proud of it. With pride I shall sleep, dress in calico, cook for myself. . . . Tell me, I can be a working woman, can't I ? If nothing else turns up I will go into a factory. . . . I am looking forward to it all so much ! "

George gazed at her with delighted astonishment. Heavens, what radiance, what courage in such a downtrodden life ! He was ashamed of his own effeminacy and weariness ; he thought of his own work with sudden warmth and happiness, infected by the ardent vitality of this strange, feverish girl. She had really become a young girl again, blushing, animated, childishly naive. Oh, it will turn out all right, how can it fail to ?

" I shall manage, you'll see," said Rosa, " I want nothing from anyone, I will support myself, and I will really earn, at least enough to provide for myself, and have a few flowers on the table. And if I had no flowers there I would go into the street and just look at them. . . . You cannot imagine how each thing has filled me with happiness since—I decided to run away. How beautifully, delightfully different everything looks! A new life has begun for me. . . . Till now I never understood how beautiful everything is. Ah, Georgie," she exclaimed with tears running down her face, "I am so happy."

"Little silly," Georgie smiled at her, delighted. "It will not be so easy. Well, we will try it. But now lie down, you mustn't make yourself ill. Don't talk to me any more now, please. I have something to think over, and in the morning I will let you know. Go to sleep now and let me think."

Nothing that he could say would induce her to take his bed; she lay down fully dressed on the sofa, he covered her with everything warm he had and turned down the lamp. It was quiet; only her rapid, childish breathing seemed to appeal to heaven for sympathy. George gently opened the window to the cool October night. The peaceful, lofty sky was bright with stars. Once in their father's house they had stood by the open window, he and little Rosa; she, shivering with cold, pressed close to him, as they waited for falling stars. "When a star falls," whispered Rosa, "I shall ask to be changed into a boy, and do something glorious." Ah, father was asleep as soundly as a log : the bed could be heard creaking under his ponderous fatigue. And George, filled with a feeling of importance, meditated on something grand and with masculine gravity protected little Rosa, who was trembling with cold and excitement.

Over the garden a star shot across the sky.

"George," Rosa's voice called him softly from the room.

"All right, directly," answered George shivering with excitement and cold.

Yes, to do something great : there was no other way out. Poor, foolish creature, what great deed did you want to do ? You have your burden to bear ; if you want to do something fine carry a greater one ; the greater your burden, the greater are you. Are you a weakling, sinking under your own burden ? Rise and help to support one who is fainting : you cannot do otherwise unless you would fall yourself.

"George," called Rosa in a hushed voice.

George turned where he stood at the window. "Listen," he began hesitatingly. "I have thought it out. . . . I think that—you will not find work to suit you. . . . There is work enough, but you will not earn enough to—oh, it's nonsense."

" I shall be satisfied with anything," said Rosa quietly.

" No, wait a moment. You really don't know what it means. You see, I have quite a fair salary now, I am glad to say, and I could get afternoon work, too. Sometimes I really do not know what to do. . . . It is quite enough for me. And I could let you have money——"

" What money ? " murmured Rosa.

" My share from our parents and the interest which has accumulated ; that makes about five thousand a year. No, not five thousand, only four. . . . It is only the interest, you understand ? It has occurred to me that I could let you have that interest, so that you might have something."

Rosa bounded off the sofa. " That is not possible," she cried excitedly.

" Don't scream," growled George. " It's only the interest, I tell you. Whenever you don't want it you need not draw it out. But now, just for the beginning. . . ."

Rosa stood like an amazed little girl. " But that will not do, what would you have ? "

" Oh, don't trouble about that," he protested.

" I have thought for a long time that I should like to get afternoon work, but—I was ashamed to take work away from my colleagues. However, you see how I live ; I shall be glad to have something to do. That's how it is ; you understand, don't you ? That money only hindered me. So now, do you want it or not ? "

" I do," sighed Rosa, approaching him on tiptoe, flinging her arms round his neck and pressing her moist little face to his. " George," she whispered, " I never dreamed of this ; I swear to you that I wanted nothing from you, but since you are so good——"

" Never mind," he said, deeply stirred. " That's beside the point. That money really does not matter to me, Rosa ; when a man is fed up with life, he must do something. . . . But what can one do all alone ? In spite of all efforts one can only come face to face with oneself again in the end ; you know, it is like living surrounded by nothing but mirrors, and whenever one looks in them there is only one's own face, one's own boredom, one's own loneliness. . . . If you knew what that means ! No, Rosa, I do not want to tell you about myself, but I am so glad that you are here, so glad that this has happened. Look how many stars there are : do you remember how once at home we watched for falling stars ? "

" No, I don't remember," said Rosa, turning a pale face to his ; in the dim frosty light he saw her eyes shining like stars. " Why are you like this ? "

He thrilled with pleasant excitement and stroked her hair. " Don't talk about the money. It is so dear of you to come to me. Heavens, how glad I am, as if a window had opened—among the mirrors. Can you imagine it ? I really only cared for myself. I was sick of myself, tired of myself, but I had nothing else. . . . Oh, there was no sense in it at all. Do you remember, when the stars fell, what you asked for then ? What would you ask for to-night if a star fell ? "

" What should I ask ? " Rosa smiled sweetly. " Something for myself. . . . No, something for you, for something to happen for you."

" I have nothing to wish for, Rosa, I am so glad to have got rid . . . Now, how will you arrange ? Wait, to-morrow I will find you a nice room with a pleasant outlook. From here, you only look on to the yard ; in the daytime, when there are no stars shining, it is a trifle depressing. But we must find something better for you, something more open." Quite excited and enthusiastic, he strode about the room planning out the future, eagerly picturing each new detail, laughing, talking, promising all sorts of things. . . . Of course, lodging, work, money, would all be forthcoming ; the main thing was that this would be a new life. He felt how her eyes shone in the darkness, smiling, following him with their ardent brightness ; his heart was so full that he could have laughed for joy ; he did not think of resting till, exhausted, worn out by sheer happiness and too much talking, they fell into long pauses of weariness, in utter harmony.

At last he made her lie down ; she did not resist his quaint, motherly solicitude, and could not even thank him ; but when he looked up from the piles of newspapers in which he was glancing through advertisements of lodgings and agencies, he found her eyes fixed on him with an ardent and strange brilliancy, and his heart was wrung with happiness. Thus morning found him.

Yes, it was a new life. His wretched lassitude was gone now as he swallowed a hasty dinner, then strode through countless houses in search of a room, coming home perspiring like a hunting dog and happy as a bridegroom, and settling down in the evening to plough through pieces of extra work, until he finally fell asleep worn out, and enthusiastic over a profitable

day. But he had, alas ! to put up with a room
without a pleasant outlook, a detestable room,
upholstered in plush and outrageously dear,
where he placed Rosa for the present. Sometimes, indeed, in the course of his work he was
attacked by faintness and weakness, his eyelids
would tremble, a sweat from giddiness breaking
out on his suddenly livid brow; but he
succeeded in mastering this, set his teeth and
laid his hand on the cold slab of the table,
saying resolutely : Bear it—you must bear
it—indeed, you are not living for yourself
alone. In this way he did feel better and
better as day followed day. This was a new
life.

Suddenly one day he had an unexpected
visit. It was his other sister Tylda ; she was
married to a manufacturer in a small way who
was not doing well and lived some little distance out of town. She always called on him
when she came to Prague for anything—on
business trips, for she looked after everything
herself. She used regularly to sit with eyes
cast down and talk in brief, quiet phrases of
her three children and her many worries as
if there were nothing else in the world. To-
day, however, she alarmed him; she was
breathing heavily, struggling in her cobweb
of ceaseless cares, and her fingers, disfigured
by writing and sewing, touched his heart and

made it ache with sympathy. Thank heaven, she got out brokenly, the children were well and good, but the workshop was not going well, machines were worn out; she was just looking for a purchaser.

"And so Rosa is here?" she suddenly said in a half-questioning tone vainly trying to raise her eyes. Strange to say, wherever her eyes rested there was a hole in the carpet, frayed furniture covers, something old, shabby, and neglected. Somehow or other neither he nor Rosa had paid any attention to such things. This vexed him, and he looked away; he was ashamed to meet her eyes, keen as needles and relentless as unceasing care.

"She has run away from her husband," she began indifferently. "Says that he plagued her. Perhaps he did, but everything has a cause."

"He had cause, too," she went on, failing to provoke questions. "You see, Rosa is— I don't know how to put it . . . " She was silent, stitching with heavy eyes at a large hole in the carpet. "Rosa isn't a housewife," she began after a time. "And, of course, she has no children, need not work, has no cares, but——"

George looked gloomily out of the window.

"Rosa is a spendthrift," Tylda forced out of herself. "She has run him into debt, you see. . . . Have you noticed what her linen is like ? ”

“ No.”

Tylda sighed and made as if wiping something from her forehead. “ You’ve no idea what it costs. . . . She buys, say, furs, for thousands, and then sells them for a few hundred to pay for boots. She used to hide the bills from him : then there came summonses. . . . Do you know about this ? ”

“ No. He and I are not on speaking terms.”

Tylda nodded. “ He is queer, of course, I don’t dispute it. . . . But when she does not mend a scrap of linen for him, and when she herself goes about like a duchess—tells him lies—and carries on with other men——”

“ Stop,” begged George in anguish.

Tylda’s sad eyes mended a torn bed cover. “ Perhaps she has offered you,” she asked uncertainly, “ to housekeep for you ? Suggested your taking larger lodgings—and that she should cook for you ? ”

George’s heart contracted painfully. This had never occurred to him. Nor had it to Rosa. Heavens, how happy he would be ! “ I should not want her to,” he said sharply, controlling himself by main force.

Tylda succeeded in raising her eyes. “ Perhaps she would not want it either. She has got him here—her officer. They transferred him to Prague. That's why she ran away—and has taken up with him—a married man. Of course, she has said nothing about it to you."

"Tylda," he said, hoarsely, withering her with his glance, "you lie."

Her hands and face quivered, but she would not give in yet. "See for yourself," she stammered. "You are too kind-hearted. I would not have said this if—if I were not sorry for you. Rosa never cared for you. She said you were——"

"Go!" he cried, beside himself with rage. "For God's sake leave me in peace!"

Tylda rose slowly. "You should—you should get better lodgings, George," she said with dignified calm. "Look how dirty this place is. Would you like me to send you a little box of pears?"

"I don't want anything."

"I must be off. . . . How dark it is here. . . . Dear, dear, George; well, good-bye, then."

The blood throbbed in his temples, his throat contracted; he tried to work, but he had only just sat down when he broke his pen in a rage, sprang to his feet and hurried round to see Rosa. He ran to her place in a sweat and rang: the landlady opened the door, and said that the young lady had been out since the morning : was there any message ?

"It doesn't matter," growled George, and shuffled home as though carrying an immense load. There he sat down to his papers, leaned his head on his hand and began to study ; but an hour went by and he had not turned over a page ; dusk was followed by darkness, and he did not light up. Then the bell rang in a breezy, cheery way, there was a rustle of skirts in the passage and Rosa flew into the room. "You are asleep, Georgie ? " She smiled tenderly. "Why, how dark it is here ; where are you ? "

"Eh ? I have been busy," he remarked drily. There was an air of chilliness in the room and an exceedingly pleasant scent.

"Listen," she began cheerfully.

"I wanted to go round to you," he interrupted, "but I thought perhaps you would not be at home."

"Why, where should I have been ? " she asked in genuine wonder. "Oh, how nice it is here. Georgie, I am so glad to be with you." Joy and youth breathed from her and she was radiant with happiness. "Come and sit by me," she said, and when he was seated beside her on the sofa she slipped her arm round his neck and repeated, "I am so happy, Georgie." He rested his face again her cold fur, bedewed with autumn mist, let himself be rocked gently, and thought : Suppose she has been somewhere, what is that to me, after all ? At any rate, she has come back to me at once. But his heart grew faint and oppressed with a strange mixture of keen pain and a sweet odour.

" What is the matter, Georgie ? " she cried in shrill alarm.

" Nothing," he said as though lulled. " Tylda has been here."

" Tylda," she repeated, dismayed. " Let go of me," she said, after a while. " What did she say ? "

" Nothing."

" Come now, she spoke of me, didn't she ? Did she say anything horrid ? "

" Well, yes—a few things."

Rosa burst into wrathful tears. " The nasty creature. She is always jealous of everything I have. How can I help it if things go badly with them ? She must have come because— because she found out what you had been doing for me. If things went better with them, she would forget all about you. It is so disgusting. She wants everything for herself—for her children—those horrid children."

" Don't talk about it," entreated George.

But Rosa went on crying. " She wants to spoil everything for me. I have scarcely begun to have a happier life when she comes along, slandering me and waiting to take things from me. Tell me, do you believe what she has been saying ? "

" No."

" I really want nothing more than to be free. Haven't I a right then to be a little more happy ? I want so little, and was so happy here, George, and then she comes along——"

" Don't worry about that," he said, and went to light the lamp. Rosa stopped crying at once. He looked at her closely, as though for the first time. She was looking at the floor, her lips were trembling. Ah, how pretty and youthful ! She had on new clothes, small gloves, so close-fitting that they seemed ready to burst ; and silk stockings peeped from under her skirt. Her little nervous hands played with the threads of the worn sofa-covering.

" Excuse me," he said sighing. " I have some work to do just now."

She obeyed and rose. " Ah, Georgie," she began, and did not know how to go on. With hands clasped against her breast, she gave him a swift, agonized glance and stood there, white-lipped, like an image of fear. " Don't be anxious," he said briefly, and turned to his work.

Next day he was sitting over his papers until twilight. He compelled himself to work mechanically, smoothly and unheedingly, and forced himself to go quicker and quicker; but all the time he was working there grew and deepened within him a keen sense of pain. Presently Rosa came in. "Go on writing," she whispered. "I shall not disturb you." She sat down quietly on the sofa, but he felt that her passionate, sleep-robbed, vigilant eyes never left him.

"Why didn't you come to me?" she burst out suddenly. "I was at home to-day." He felt in this a confession which touched him. He laid down his pen and turned to her; she was dressed in black like a penitent, paler than usual, folded in her lap were her appealing little hands, which even from where he sat he felt must be cold.

"It is rather chilly there," he observed apologetically, and tried to talk as usual without making reference to the happenings of the previous day. She replied humbly and gently like a grateful child.

"About Tylda, you know," the words came all at once, "the reason things go so badly with them is that her husband is a duffer. He stood surety for someone and then had to pay. . . . It is his own fault, and he ought to have thought of his children; but then, he doesn't understand anything. He had an agent who robbed him, and yet goes on trusting everyone. You know they are suing him for fraudulent bankruptcy ? "

" I know nothing about it," George turned it off: he saw that she had been brooding over it all night, and felt somehow ashamed. Rosa was not aware of his quiet rebuff: she lost her temper, got excited, and immediately played her highest card : " They wanted my husband to help them, but he obtained information and simply laughed at them outright. To give them money, he said, would be to throw it away ; they have three hundred thousand of liabilities. . . . A man would be a fool to put a single heller into that : he would lose it all."

" Why do you tell me this ? "

" So that you might know," she forced herself to a gentle tone. " You know you are so kind-hearted, you would very likely let yourself be deprived of everything."

" You are very kind," he said without taking his eyes from her. She was highly strung, burning with desire to say something more, but his scrutiny made her uneasy ; she began to be afraid that she had gone too far. She asked him to find her some work so that she might be a burden to no one, no one at all ; she could live with strictly limited expenditure ; she felt she ought not to have such expensive lodgings. . . . Now at last perhaps she would offer to housekeep for him. He waited with beating heart, but she looked away towards the window and began on something else.

The next day he received the following letter from Tylda :

DEAR GEORGE,

I am sorry we parted under such a misunderstanding. If you knew all I am sure you would read this letter differently. We are in a desperate position. If we succeeded in paying off that fifty thousand we should be saved, for our business has a future, and in two years it would begin to pay. We would give you every guarantee for the future if you would let us have the money now. You would be part proprietor of the works and take a share of the proceeds as soon as the business began to pay. If you will come and look at our establishment you will see for yourself that it has a future. You will also get to know our children better, and see how nice and good they are and so diligent, and you will not have the heart to ruin their whole future. Do it, at least, for the children, for they are of our blood, and Charles is already big and intelligent and gives promise of a great future. Forgive me for writing this, we are in a fine flutter and are quite sure that you will come to our rescue and become fond of our children, for you have a kind heart. Be sure and come. When little Tylda is grown up she will be glad to be housekeeper to her uncle, you will see what a darling she is. If you don't help us my husband will never get over it and these children will be beggars.

Kind love, dear George, from your unhappy sister,

TYLDA.

P.S.—With regard to Rosa, you said that I told lies. When my husband comes to Prague he will bring you proofs. Rosa does not deserve your support and generosity, for she has brought shame on us. She had better go back to her husband, he will forgive her, and she ought not to rob innocent children of their bread.

George flung the letter aside. He felt bitter and disgusted, the unfinished work on his table presented an air of hopeless triviality. Disgust rose in a painful lump in his throat; he left everything and went round to Rosa. He was already on the steps before her door when he changed his mind with a sudden jerk of his hand, came down again, and strolled aimlessly about the street. He saw in the distance a young woman in furs on an officer's arm; he started running after them like a jealous lover, but it was not Rosa. He saw a pair of bright eyes in a woman's face, heard a laugh on rosy lips, saw the woman radiating and exhaling happiness, full of trust and joy and beauty. Wearily he returned home at last. On his sofa lay Rosa in tears. Tylda's open letter fell to the floor.

"Miserly creature," she sobbed passionately, " and not ashamed of herself. She wants to rob you of everything, Georgie; don't give her anything, don't believe a word of it. You can't understand what a crafty, avaricious woman she is. Why does she pursue me like that? What have I done to her? For the sake of your money—to slander me in that way! It is only—only because of your money. It is really monstrous!"

" She has children, Rosa," George observed gently.

" That is her own look-out," she cried fiercely, choking with sobs. " She has always robbed us and only cares for money. She married for money, even when she was little she boasted that she would be rich. She is absolutely disgusting, vulgar, stupid—tell me, Georgie, what is there in her? You know what she was like when things went better with them—fat, insolent, unfriendly. And now she wants—to rob me. . . . George, would you let her? Would you get rid of me? I would rather drown myself than go back."

George listened with bowed head. Yes, this girl was fighting for everything, for her love and happiness; she wept with rage, she cried out in passionate hatred against everyone, against Tylda, and even against himself who could take everything from her. Money—the word stung George like a whip whenever she said it; it struck him as shameless, disgusting, offensive.

"It was like a miracle to me when you offered me money," wept Rosa. "It meant for me freedom—everything. You offered it yourself, Georgie, and you should not have offered it at all if you meant to take it away again. Now, when I am counting on it——"

George was no longer listening. Remotely he heard reproaches, lamentations, sobs. He felt humiliated beyond measure. Money, money, but was it only a question of money? O God, how had it come about? What had coarsened the careworn, motherly Tylda. Why was the other sister wailing? Why had his own heart grown hard and indifferent? What had money to do with it at all? In a strange way he was aware of his power to hurt Rosa, and of an inexplicable desire to wound her by saying something cruel, humiliating, and masterful.

He rose with a certain lightness. "Wait," he said coldly. "It is my own money. And I," he concluded with a magnificent gesture of dismissal, "shall think it over."

Rosa sprang up with eyes full of alarm. "You—you——" she stammered. "But at all events—that's understood. Please, Georgie —perhaps you did not understand me—I didn't mean that——"

" All right," he broke in drily. " I say I shall think it over."

A gleam of hatred blazed in Rosa's eyes ; but she bit her lip, and went out with bowed head.

Next day there was a new visitor waiting in his room : Tylda's husband, an awkward, blushing man, full of embarrassment and dog-like submissiveness. George, choking with shame and fury, refrained from sitting down, so as to compel his visitor to stand.

" What is your business ? " he said, in the impersonal tone of an official.

The awkward man shivered and forced out of himself : " I —I—that is, Tylda—has sent some documents—which you asked for——" and began to hunt feverishly in his pockets.

" I certainly did not ask for any papers," said George with a negative wave of his hand. There was a painful pause.

" Tylda wrote to you, brother-in-law," began the unfortunate tradesman, blushing more than ever, " that our business, to put it shortly, if you would like to be a partner——"

George purposely let him flounder.

" The fact is—things are not so bad, and if you were a partner, to put it shortly, our undertaking has a future, and as one who . . . shared——"

The door opened softly and there stood Rosa.

She became petrified at the sight of Tylda's husband.

" What is the matter ? " said George sharply.

" Georgie," gasped Rosa.

" I am engaged," George rebuffed her, and turned to his guest. " I beg your pardon."

Rosa did not stir.

Tylda's husband perspired with shame and terror. " Here are—please—these proofs, letters which her husband wrote us and other papers intercepted——"

Rosa clutched at the door for support. " Show me them," said George. He took the letters and feigned to read the first, but then crushed them all in his hand and gave them to Rosa. " There you are," he smiled malevolently. " And now excuse me. And don't go to the bank to draw anything out : you would go for nothing."

Rosa retreated without a word, her face ashen.

" Well now, your business," continued George hoarsely, closing the door.

" Yes, the prospects are—of the very best, and if there were capital—that is, of course, without interest——"

" Listen," George interrupted unceremoniously. " I know that you are to blame ; I am informed that you are not provident or— businesslike——"

"I would do my best," stammered Tylda's husband, gazing at him with pleading, dog-like eyes, from which George turned away.

"How can I put any confidence in you?" he asked, shrugging his shoulders.

"I assure you—that I would value your confidence—and all that is possible—we have children, brother-in-law."

A terrible, intense, embarrassing feeling of sympathy wrung George's heart. "Come in a year's time," he finished, holding on to the last fragment of his shattered will.

"In a year's time . . . Oh God . . ." groaned Tylda's husband, and his pale eyes filled with tears.

"Good-bye," said George, extending his hand.

Tylda's husband did not see the proffered hand. He made for the door and stumbled over a chair, groping vainly for the door-knob. "Good-bye," he said in a broken voice at the door, "and—thank you."

George was alone. A sweat of intense weakness burst out on his forehead. He arranged the papers on his table once more and called the landlady; when she arrived he was pacing the room with both hands pressed to his heart; he forgot what he wanted her for.

"Stop," he cried, as she was going out, "if to-day, to-morrow, or at any time my sister

Rosa comes, tell her that I am not well and that . . . I would rather not see anyone."

Then he stretched himself on his old sofa, fixing his eyes on a new spider's web freshly spun in the corner above his head.

HELENA

At the watering-place he met her, this tall, striking-looking, raw-boned, long-legged girl. She had beautiful grey eyes, features fine drawn and cheeks curved only to the firmer mould within. She held herself erect, but her movements were ill-defined; half boy and half nymph, full of timidity and a most puzzling bashfulness; she was, in short, a type which captivated him especially in these surroundings of summer woods, sunny languor and mental repose to which he had abandoned himself. She was a student of some sort, " arts," perhaps; she had her " opinions " according to which she thought and observed, a dash of pedantry, and much more education than the average; she wore frocks with large pockets in which she tucked away her books. Her store of learning seasoned with a certain boyish candour the reserved chaste maturity of a strong introspective woman. In speaking of learned Pallas, forget not her divine virginity.

They became friends easily, amused perhaps

by each other's peculiarities. He felt that this wise virgin was making efforts to read him as though he were a new, significant book, but he found it rather pleasant. There are women who have a craze for regarding human beings as psychological novels, bless them, they seek to classify people, try to read their souls, judge of them profoundly and with singular cocksureness, and in the end arrive at judgments that are either just plain injustices, or immensely complicated tangles of error. In her errors Helena was mysteriously complicated. This man with whom she went strolling in the forest, who was fond of talking, contemptuous of many things, and amused with all, of impetuous mind, intelligent, sceptical, was for her, goodness knows why, a being after the style of Hamsun's Falk. At home she analysed him, full of profound and not very clear perceptions; meanwhile he was bored, or slept, finding in himself less of piquant interest than in a grain of snuff.

Their walks together, however, were quite another matter. Now Helena had no leisure to think about him; she listened, her pretty eyes gazing ahead, her attention held by his restless animation. At times, gently and hesitatingly, her own voice made itself heard; she did not know that to him it rang with melodious clearness in tune with the manifold accompaniment of nature's music. She did not know that with her serious voice and boyish face, with her coarse, severely cut dress, she was cleanly and crudely pleasing to him, a cheery note of purity and harmony, a note of Pallas at large among the woods, the sun-light and the elements. She was not aware of all this, but she had a feeling never experienced before that she was pretty; oh, but never did she resuscitate this feeling before her mirror at home, though here in the forest she sensed it with blushing delight. The delight was the greater, when he, a sceptic, told her that there was a better sentiment than love between man and woman; there are wells of harmony which are infinitely broader and more natural. For these words Helena gratefully wanted to give him her hand, but was shy on account of this same hand which she thought too large, and which accordingly she continued to conceal in her glove. Scarcely breathing a word she walked along by his side, wondering at herself that she found such pleasure in being just a girl; there stirred in her, strange to say, not the slightest motion of revolt against the self-evident masculine superiority. It was a charming and memorable day. Helena, relieved of the burden of artificially main-tained pride, felt herself drawn by a strange feeling of comradeship to this man who gave her back the pleasure of being a young girl.

Very soon Helena was put to a somewhat searching test. There came to the resort a young married woman of rounded figure, creamy complexion, and exuberant charms; on the very first evening she picked on Helena's friend and gave him clearly to understand that he would not love her in vain. This did not escape Helena, but there was, of course, no question of jealousy, good heavens no, but all at once she became stiff, restrained, ugly and almost foolishly awkward; when he directed the conversation towards her she replied disagreeably and as though irritated. She hated herself for this cruel suffering and bravely she controlled herself; that night she was almost in tears, but then she became convinced that he was nothing but a braggart, a self-indulgent idler, a common-place egoist; with this consolation she fell asleep happily. She went out earlier in the morning in order not to meet him, and climbed the wooded height at the summit of which they had "discovered" a huge stone seat, with a passably pretty view of the watering-place. She sat there, filled with a spirit of sacred solitude, experiencing to the full the peace of exalted abnegation, she pardoned the whole world. But look there! was not that yesterday's braggart climbing up the sunny path through the flowering brambles and verbascum? She wanted to run away, but only offended Pallas ran away; Helena stayed, and in spite of all she could do her eyes filled with tears. She turned away lest he should see, lest he should look into her eyes, and above all because to-day she was not at all pretty. He sat down and talked, but not a word that anything had gone wrong or that he was seeking her to offer an explanation of any sort: but he spoke gravely and did not force her to be cheerful. And thus, blazing noon found them together on that stone seat in friendly conversation, which meant simply that everything was completely and utterly right. Down below, across the town square, there floated a white blob with a red parasol: perhaps it was the blonde beauty. Yes, it was midday and the man knew very well that a long, long time had passed since they should have gone down; must he then sit there until evening? Helena sat there with her long hands pressed between her knees and smiled, not with her lips, nor even with her eyes, but in her mind.

" How late is it ? " she asked at length.

" Two o'clock," replied the man, controlling himself with superhuman efforts so as not to sound discontented.

But what were hours to Helena? In truth "there is a higher feeling than love," and Helena felt herself infinitely above love and passion: never, never would she know weakness. At last she rose; on the way back she picked a few flowers, and put them in her belt, she meant to keep them as relics. The man sighed: it is not very easy to perform an act of charity. They descended at four o'clock, which was a notable scandal in the life of the watering-place.

Undisturbed days followed, when they went out together with joy unspoilt. God scattered discoveries and adventures along their paths; they found nesting birds, or scared a sitting hare; then on a blazing hot afternoon they sat by a deserted rural bowling alley, in solemn silence they sat amidst hens and chickens; another day they were overtaken in the fields by a heavy shower which drove them, happy couple, to seek shelter in a low straw-thatched hut, deserted for the season by its youthful guardian of the fruit crop; a rainbow raised before them a magic triumphal arch; one morning they came upon a family of deer at pasture in a forest clearing; they knew where amongst the young trees unknown to all the world there grew a mushroom of record size. They buried in another place a dead goldfinch, found encian and charming cyclamen, came across an old woman whom they asked for milk and who delighted Helena by calling her "young madam." There were countless adventures and happenings which they lived through together and for which they were equally grateful. Helena accepted as her own all his boyish delights, enlivened by a double pleasure, the pleasure of something new and the pleasure of companionship in interest. They thoroughly agreed in everything that pleased him. She said "our cyclamen" though it was he who found it; everything was his doing, everything passed at first through his eyes and flowed from his wealth: poor Helena, where was your share in this joint world? Ah, Helena did not know, but smiled with downcast eyes; her share was this harmony, her merit was great, her heart clean and humble: it just happened that he discovered everything, and she made of it mutual delight and fulness of harmony.

So, good-bye for to-day, Helena, to-morrow we shall go somewhere else and thanks to you for the happiness of to-day.

.   .   .   .   .

He went away and Helena wrote to him; at first he was startled by her crude, inelegant, too large handwriting; he perceived in her violent feelings hitherto unnoticed. Her style struck him as artificial, her cheerfulness forced ; he did not see why he must read about encian now withered or about the finding of the bones of a dog in " our quarry." It is strange how little survives of the most beautiful harmony when people are no longer together.

Helena in turn came back to town in the autumn, and lost much, very much, on the soil of Prague. He liked well enough to walk with her on the outskirts of Prague where there was in progress a minute, detailed struggle between the land and the town. Incomparable occasions these, full of desolation and weariness when one seemed to wander over a now hushed battle-field, the earth wounded and the town expiring in a mass of debris. Then, too, there are areas of great simplicity, like the White Mountain and the river, beautiful and mysterious beyond all rivers in the world. There are the morning hours, most precious of all, and all unknown to town-dwellers. Sailing thus early in the morning in a small steamer against the stream, so intimate are the voices heard that you would not believe human habitations can be so near.

One morning they went together along the Bránik towing-path. It was a silvery-grey autumn day, the Vltava a stream of light and of soft metallic murmurs. There was in all these surroundings much unusual tranquillity, and, so much of soothed grief, that involun-

tarily he began to speak of himself. He talked
of all he had wished to be and what he had not
become, when he had wanted to do and what
had escaped him; he complained of himself
and, abandoning all reserve, poured out all his
discontent in one unbroken torrent. He felt
that by his confession he was ridding himself
of all diffidence and weakness. It seemed to
him that he was in truth regarding this stony
towing-path from afar, from the opposite
bank of the broad river; here walking along-
side the stream were two people, utterly
insignificant in the presence of the river, the
plain and the sky; they only emphasized the
loneliness and forlornness of the universe. It
was infinitely more solitary than in the depths
of the summer woods.

" Helena," he said, " why, this is not life at
all. It is a growing old, a dullness, a passing of
time, or what you like, but it is not life. I am
good for nothing and can do nothing : but
if I start doing something I feel in advance, why
on earth do I ? Of course I myself have nothing
from it. I myself ! I myself ! My whole life
long I have thought only of myself, but,
behold ! nothing, as a matter of fact, have I
ever done for myself. That is not life. Help
yourself, man ! But how can an egoist help
himself ? Helena, I have gone through many
experiences, but the saddest of all is to feel

one's own weakness. I am tired of so many things. You are listening to all this, and it is all so worthless. Your patience astounds me. Look there, what a large fish that man has caught."

He pointed with his finger. Helena raised her downcast eyes, but not to follow his finger ; she beamed brightly on him. This full glance perplexed him and, not knowing how to continue, he toned down what he had just said, went into details and finally started to jest. Helena, however, was so absorbed in her own thoughts that she did not speak and would not listen. The walk finished almost out of humour. On the steamer they did not speak : he was rather bored and glad to say good-bye. The rest of that day is of no importance : early on the morrow brought him a letter from Helena. His heart full of misgivings he opened the envelope.

"While it is still to-day," began the letter in agitated script, "I must thank thee, dear, my dearest. . . ."

He put down the letter as if struck, this sudden "thee," this "dearest" . . . had the girl taken leave of her senses ? He walked up and down the room, this needed getting accustomed to. He felt ashamed and humiliated and wanted to sink through the floor. What next ?

While it is still to-day I must thank thee, dear, my dearest, for the most beautiful day of my life. You have given me all, you have given me love. Until yesterday I lived through a weary dream which was not life. To-day I stand at the window with open arms, is it thee, is it thee for whom I extend them, my dearest, is it thee ? I know I am mad, and that perhaps in a very little time I shall be sorry for what I have written to thee. I hasten with all speed to tell all before that time of regret arrives for rather would I regret than not have said it. I kiss thee, I kiss thee, my dear, do not question me because I do not know what is happening to me it was not life but a terrible dream, my dear thank you thank you I am thine, and want nothing else. Jesus, do not prevent me from saying everything. I wish I could embrace thy feet, throw all my body beneath thee because I am so much thine already that there is nothing else I can do bear me up my darling, I have no power, I place my head on thy shoulder and oh kiss me, does thou not know, cruel one, that no one has even kissed me ? Ah, if I were only with thee !

HELENA.

Dear dearest, I am afraid of evening. Give me thy hand think of me, it is my first night !

He read in pained alarm, inexorably noting every error of punctuation, every desperate incoherence of the foolish letter. His feeling of shame increased. What have I done,

he reflected, how have I caused this ? Heavens !
Did I, perhaps, make love to her yesterday ?
What is wrong with her ? Is it really a fit of
hysteria ? Perhaps it is intended for someone
else, it occurred to him. And hastily he looked
through the crazy letter again. Unfortunately
there was no doubt about it : the " darling "
is I myself. When did I speak to her of love,
when did I tell her a lie ? Certainly she pleased
me but solely for the one simple reason that
there was no question at all of love. . . .
Heavens, what has gone wrong ?

He read her letter through once more, and
felt in it her feverish panting breath. Savage,
mad, must have been the struggle of that manly
maiden before she lost her head. But, he
paused in evil suspicion, was there such a
struggle after all ? Perhaps she was only
waiting for my first weakness to throw her
hysterical arms around me. Of course, I did
complain and groan ; a fine opportunity, by
jove, for her to unload on me her burthen-
some virginity. Ah, Helena, he trembled,
forgive me, you did not do that. You wanted
to help me, one of the disappointed, you wanted
in some way to sacrifice yourself, to do something great. Silly child, how did you imagine
such a thing ?

Once again he scrutinized her letter, more
and more repulsive it seemed to him. The

writing is all awry, written in the twilight, the
hand wet with perspiration, evidently a crisis.
There is sign or shadow neither of calculation
nor of magnanimous and foolish sacrifice.
She wanted kisses, aye, and more than kisses.
She is twenty-five years old. The revolt of
nature is powerful and terrible. He recalled
her Pallas-like figure, the sexless purity of
womanhood not yet in bloom. A something, a
taint fell upon her. Poor Helena, if you were
at least beautiful no one would be surprised
at your passion and you would not be degraded
in anybody's eyes. But you are not beautiful,
and there is nothing left but to be unjust to
you. Go! Helena; if anything is certain on
this earth it is that I do not love you.

Again he thought of her, thought kindly of
her and seemed to see her clear benignant eyes.
No, Helena, wise maiden, I do not believe
even that; it is no regular movement of
nature, no carnal revolt of the flesh, but some
extraordinary mistake. Your heart is confused,
to-morrow it will be calm and settled, but alas,
you will remember what you have done and
it will be a dreadful shame and humiliation
to you. You will despise yourself and be in
an agony of fiery shame. You will never, never
want to set eyes on me again. Helena, how
can I tell you this? Do not think about it,
I knew at once that things were not so. I have

burnt the letter and thrown away the ashes and now I do not know what was wirtten in it; obviously something to say that you love me the most noble way.

He rushed to the table and began to write . . .

Thanks for the words of love: I feel myself unworthy. Thou givest me more than my poor heart can ever repay. I am a worn-out man, my little girl, and the world has not made me as good as thou deservest.

And now, dear Helena, we can be wise once more. You have spoken the word that had to be spoken: You are brave and wonderful. It was indeed necessary that we should sincerely . . .

He put down the pen. It is still quite clear that I do not love her: how is it possible not to say so? Mechanically he scribbled on the writing pad the word " never " and then the bell rang. He heard the servant open the outer door; someone quietly spoke and knocked on his door. He called " come in," but no one entered. He went and opened it himself; Helena was leaning against the doorpost pressing both her large hands to her breast.

" Come in, please," he said with set teeth and shut the door behind her, then as he wrung his hands, " How could you, Helena, how could you ? "

Helena looked aside, her lips were trembling

painfully. "I came to tell thee . . ." she began.

"I know what you want to say," he broke in desperately. "Sit down, Helena."

With downcast eyes she sat down on the edge of the sofa and crushed her bag in her fingers. "I have come to ask you to give me back that letter."

"I had just started to write to you," he answered quietly. "What a fright you gave me."

She turned to him, eyes full of despair.

"Now, Helena," he said softly, "how did you sleep?"

She stood up, threw away her bag, took off her hat and removed her coat. The awful part of it all was that he had not asked her to do this. The garment was caught on some button, and with her trembling fingers she could not unfasten it, but he did not move to help her. She pulled violently, and blindly, and something ripped: she let the coat fall, he bent down quickly to lift it up, and then she grasped his head with both hands.

With a jerk he straightened himself, his eyes dark with hatred; but as she held him convulsively, she staggered at this movement and would have fallen; he had to catch her with both arms. Then her hands loosened, he felt her fingers quiver on his face with caressing, burning agitation as she fell with all her weight into his embrace : her head thrown back, her eyes closed, dry lips offered themselves to him as in a last kiss above the exposed and chattering teeth, the point of her tongue trembling between them, her face grey-pale and feverish ; thus she upraised her face to him in the horror of passionate longing. She was almost ugly ; everything was extinguished in that face when the eyes were closed. He breathed a sibilant sound of disgust and kissed her lightly on the face ; tenderly, most tenderly, he removed her hands from his face and said with ponderous melancholy, " Sit down, Helena."

Although intoxicated, she sat down and covered her face with her hands.

" Helena," he said brokenly, walking across the room, " I do not want this meeting to cause you any after regrets, I beg of you to be sensible. I do not recognize you, God knows, I do not understand you at all ; but I am afraid that to-morrow you will think reproachfully of me."

Helena sat there stonily.

" Forgive me," he went on bitterly, " for thinking to-day about to-morrow. It would be better if there were no to-morrow. Say, are you certain that to-morrow will not revenge itself upon you ? "

Helena, with face covered, shook her head.

"You came to put yourself into my hands; here I am, do as you will with me. But girl, how is it possible? Am I to hold you, to embrace you, to take possession of you? How can I know in what way I shall injure you the most? Ah, Helena, spare me this, I beseech you; do not ask me to decide what to do with you; my will is gone, but I am fond of you. Pull yourself together, Helena."

She sat there dumb, motionless, rigid; he was intensely sorry for her and anxiously sought for the tenderest words in which to explain the state of affairs. So as to be nearer to her, he sat on the head of the sofa and looked down on her coarse hair.

"Now look here," he repeated gently, "pull yourself together. You are pure and proud, do not lower yourself. I know you too little; I have a feeling that to-day is sent to us by fate that I may begin to esteem you infinitely more highly than hitherto. Helena, I delighted in you as an innocent girl; I will respect you as a woman who has conquered herself. You will be sure of yourself and forget."

Then Helena did something unexpected and very simple. As he sat above her with his knees raised, she uncovered her face and placed her chin on his knee with a movement inexpressibly childlike and winsome; in that position she became motionless and closed her eyes as though she would say: "Now talk as you like."

He was confused, for he felt himself full well the falsity of all that he was saying.

"Helena," he began again sadly. "Is it a great fault that I am not young enough to believe in love? Is it a great fault that when I hear the word *love* I think at once of pain and disappointment, crude sensuality, the vilest contacts, falsehood and a parting? Is it a great fault?"

With closed eyes Helena shook her head. He felt at his knee the violent beating of the artery in her throat; pale and as if asleep she breathed rapidly through parted lips. "Now," seemed to say this coaxing face at this moment, "all is one to me, let me stay thus." She almost became beautiful in this motionless attitude: she looked like an ivory mask. He bent over her and said in a low tone: "Helena, it is not love that you should desire, it is tiresome and always degrading: it is not for you. If I ever saw you tread that path with another, whoever he might be, I would call to you in terror: 'Helena, Helena, do not go that way, it is not for you; you cannot cross where others walk, what they can endure would crush you ; I do not know whether it is because you are more wise or more unhappy.' I do not profess to understand you, but I am afraid for you. What more can I say to you ? "

Helena's cheeks were slightly tinged with red. She looked strangely charming, her features grew tender, she looked out mysteriously, in no particular direction, through eyelids that formed narrow slits. He stroked her hair and said softly :

" Helena, you must not come to me again."

Not a quiver crossed her face, she would have endured any blow, it seemed, in that position. He sighed and touched her face.

" Good-bye, Helena."

Obediently she stood up and allowed her coat to be put on. He helped to put in her hat-pin and she smiled at him.

Having moved away, she turned vehemently and shook his hand with all her strength, " you . . . are . . . so . . . noble," she said, blushing, with downcast eyes, as though thanking him that she had come to no harm. In spite of himself he was compelled to bite his lips.

From that day they never met again ; it was really impossible that they should.

In after years he heard of Helena again. He

learnt that she spoke of him with evident animosity as of one who had done her a grievous wrong.

He was sorry for that, even after years had passed.

THREE

THE sun, which since early morning had been scorching the yellow walls of the farmyards opposite, slowly advanced in grim silence. The walls opposite were already in shadow, and it seemed really as if this made it a little cooler. Now a narrow streak of sunlight lodged on the window-frame, presently it would broaden, and when it fell across the room her husband would wake up, yawn noisily and come in to her, just as he did every Sunday. Marie shrugged her shoulders in dreary disgust and dropped her sewing into her lap.

She stared vacantly out of the window. The chestnut in the court had flowered not long before, but now the blossom had a look as if corroded. Why was it that even the tree filled her with disgust, when it at least was not to blame? A restless, ever increasing, grievous heaviness descended on Marie's heart. If she had wished to talk about herself she might have said that perhaps it was memories ; but she never talked about herself, not even to her husband, not even to the other one. However, it was not even memories. It was only as if all the past had rolled into a heavy ball of thread; she had only to pick up the end and one event after another, those which she would gladly recall to life for her own pleasure, and those which she wanted to forget for ever, began to unroll. Marie was thinking of nothing, she did not want to think of anything, but she was conscious of everything about which she might be thinking now. It was all there, and so close that she was afraid to think lest she should touch it.

The little streak of sunshine had jumped across the window-frame.

Above all there was the helpless consciousness that everyone knew about it—everyone knew all about her conjugal infidelity. Oh, at first she had borne it defiantly when so many people made it quite clear to her that they knew. . . . Some of them did it brutally, others with offensive familiarity, others wishing to chastise, and still others—why, there was not one who did not feel she had the right to say something nasty to her. One neighbour muttered audibly something about light women whenever she met her; another shook her head and declared that young people must have their fling, what was the use of being virtuous; another kept making meaning allusions to her husband; another spat; another did not acknowledge her greeting; another overflowed with shrill sympathy and then proceeded to borrow all manner of things. Oh God, must she bear all this?

Yes, at first Marie had forced herself to be defiant, but it is hard to defy one's own evil conscience. And then she shed tears of rage and indignation, but without relief. She could not even complain to her lover, she had never anything to say to him herself; she was kept a speechless captive by the silent, heavy and masterful love of a clumsy and passionate man. Finally she took to pretending that she did not understand the allusions, that they did not refer to her; one gets accustomed to anything, though this "anything" does not thereby become purified, changed or undone.

The ray of sunshine glided down the cords of the blinds.

And then there was her husband. At first perhaps he had not believed what people said about his wife; then he was seized by harrowing despair, and without saying a word to her he took to drink. He became a dreadful drinker, he who had been so temperate a man, and went down in a pitiable way; at last, in the office they threatened to retire him, so he changed abruptly, gave up drinking, and began again in his old way, becoming even more economical and stay-at-home than before. For a long time he said nothing to Marie, but finally he had to discuss expenses, laundry, food. . . . He became particular about his food and grew miserly, after he " reformed "; he exacted much consideration and contrived to be content with that. Once he found Baudys, Marie's lover, at his house; he banged the door and without looking at anybody, went into the other room; but as soon as the visitor had gone he allowed himself to be called to supper; he did not speak at first, but after the meal he began to talk about something or other with painful pauses, like a man who knows that he ought to be silent. Then, when Marie preferred to go to Baudys' home, he made a fuss several times because she had been out *too long*. Yes, he had had to wait for his supper. People said he was a good-natured soul. Marie hated him, partly because she was wronging him and partly because he took no trouble over himself any more.

The sunshine glided along the wall. Marie followed it like the fateful hand of a clock. She could still hear her husband snoring regularly; but after a little while the sofa in the other room would creak, her husband would yawn, get up with an effort, scratching the back of his neck, and with waistcoat unbuttoned and in his stockinged feet, come over to her as he did every Sunday. Then he would wander round the room, finger the furniture, examine damaged places which had been there for years, mutter about expenses, and then carefully and in an indirect way begin his strange weekly discourse. Marie shuddered. He had started the subject that way for a long time now. Hundreds of times he talked of how much a wife cost her husband, and what an expensive business marriage was. Bachelors get the best of it, be began one day, when they run after a married woman. Another man provides for her, another man clothes her; all that costs them nothing. A bunch of violets, perhaps, he observed, looking fixedly at Marie. They get it cheap, he repeated, dwelling on the subject, as if he had made a discovery. For a whole month he had lived on that theme, and Marie fancied he was jealous.

One day she was sewing trimming on a dress. He came up after a good sleep and asked how much the lace cost, and what was the price of one thing and another. However, he never worried her much about such things; perhaps he understood her need to be pretty; all the same he talked about it and grumbled at the cost. Nowadays, he had begun, one man alone has not enough to dress a wife; no, as things are to-day, one man alone has not a big enough income. Some men, of course, get things cheap, they get a wife for nothing as she is not theirs. . . . Marie began to understand, and it seemed to her that her heart grew cold, but she was silent as if it were nothing to do with her. Her husband looked at her with a fixed and heavy stare and burst out " How about Baudys ! " This was the first time that he had uttered the name.

" What about Baudys ? " Marie was alarmed now.

" Nothing," he said evasively, and after a time : " What—er—er income does he get ? "

That was how it began, Marie remembered. And from that time it was the same every Sunday. Why was he sleeping so long to-day ? He would come and scratch his back, " Have you spoken to Baudys ? And how often ? And what salary does he get ? " Then he would begin about himself. No money and needing a new hat—his was really a disgrace; but what could one do when housekeeping swallowed up everything ? He went on talking by himself. Disgust made a lump rise in Marie's throat which she wanted to get rid of. Her husband shook his head and ended with strange gloominess : " Of course, you don't worry yourself about anything."

Marie looked at the advancing ray of sunlight and dug her finger-nails into her palms. If she could only be spared that memory ! It

was one day at her lover's house—after such a
Sunday as this. Baudys put her on the sofa,
but she resisted him and began to cry ; she felt
it was necessary to cry, and for a long, long
time she let him beg for an explanation—that
her husband was stingy, he wouldn't give her
money for clothes or anything. Her lover
listened with a frown and as if damped ; he
was so . . . so clumsy, perhaps, that he
calculated mentally how much it would cost.
At last he said hesitatingly and reluctantly :
" I'll see to that, Marie." Marie felt that now
she could cry without pretence, but instead
she had to let herself be caressed ; oh, more
than she had, more than she had till then.

He was waiting for her next time with a gift ;
it was some dress material which Marie did not
like ; she went home feeling crushed with
shame. Up to that time her relations with her
lover had been those of a wife with her
husband ; her caresses were grave and devoted ;
now she closed her eyes on herself so as not to
shudder. While she was cutting out the
material her husband had come in. " Did
Baudys give you that ? " he asked eagerly.

Marie sighed and began to sew with long
stitches. She was sewing a silk blouse ; even
the stuff for that had been bought by her
lover. It was strange how it pleased him to
load her with costly, extravagant and tempting

presents. Sometimes she reflected happily how fond he was of her ; sometimes, however, she thought otherwise and felt terribly uneasy ; her restrained, passive love was gone ; these gifts exhaled something feverish and luxurious, and Marie forced herself into a state of unnatural and frivolous high spirits which did not itself ripen in her tranquil and healthy body. This was a fiery change which the lover received like a thirsty drunkard, but Marie as something unwelcome and repulsive. It seemed to her inexpressibly sinful, because it was against her own nature ; but she could not defend herself and swallowed it all, striving desperately and vainly not to think about it. A week ago he had tried to make her drink wine ; he himself was tipsy. She refused to drink, but when later he breathed on her with his drunken, burning, passionate breath, she could have screamed with horror.

The streak of sunlight gently settled on her mother's photograph. It was the round, clear, happy face of a countrywoman who had borne children, and with blessings in her heart rendered back to life all it had given her. Marie's hands dropped into her lap ; her husband's breathing grew quiet ; the heat was scorching and the silence very oppressive. A grunt from her husband in the next room, the sofa creaked, the floor creaked under unsteady steps. Marie began to sew rapidly. Her husband opened the door, yawned aloud, and all unbuttoned, still stupid from his sleep, perspiring, came up to her, scratching his neck. Marie did not even raise her eyes, but went on sewing more rapidly still.

Her husband wandered round the room in his stockinged feet, stood over her unsteadily, yawned, and asked:

"What's that you're sewing?"

Marie did not reply, she merely spread out her work for him to see.

"You had this from Baudys?" he asked without interest. She stuck the needle in her mouth and did not reply. Her husband sighed and fingered the silk with the air of a connoisseur, as though he understood it. "You had this from Baudys," he answered his own question.

"Ages ago," said Marie, from the corner of her mouth.

"Ah-h," yawned her husband, and began to walk about the room.

"You might at least put your shoes on," observed Marie after a time.

Her husband said nothing and continued to walk about. "Oh yes," he began, "always rags. What's the use of such nonsense. Money's nothing to you. That's what I say, Marie, money's nothing to you."

" At any rate you don't pay for it," Marie's voice was hard. She knew that the conversation was beginning as it had so many Sundays.

" I don't pay for it," repeated her husband. " Of course I don't pay for it. Where should I find the money for it ? I—have to pay for other things. I have to pay insurance premiums. . . . We haven't anything to spare for unnecessary things. You don't think of what is being paid out. A hundred and fifty for rent. And insurance. It's all one to you. Have you spoken to Baudys ? "

" Yes."

" Of course. Oh, my Lord," yawned her husband, and looked at Marie's work. " You don't think of the money, Marie. How much would that cost, that kind of material, do you know ? "

" No."

" How often have you spoken to him this week ? "

" Twice."

" Twice," he repeated thoughtfully. " It's waste of money. And you've such a lot of frocks already. Now listen, Marie."

The young woman bent her head ; now it was coming.

" For two years we haven't saved anything. It's like that, Marie. Suppose something happened, illness or anything. . . . And you think of nothing but having pretty frocks."

Marie remained obstinately silent.

"We ought to put something by; and then coal for the winter. I should be glad if I— for old age—if you had. . . . At least you might think of your own old age."

There was a torturing silence; Marie pulled her needle through the stuff hardly knowing how. Her husband gazed out of the window over her blonde head and tried to say something; his wretched unshaven chin, stained from a meal, was trembling.

"Stop!" cried Marie.

His chin fell; he gave a helpless gulp and said: "You know, I could do with some clothes myself; but I know that we haven't the money to spend on them. That's how it is, Marie."

He sat down, huddled up, and stared at the floor.

Marie stuck her needle into the silk. Yes, a week ago he had talked like that; she herself could have wept over his shabby clothes. She turned them over every day, was familiar with each frayed thread; she was ashamed when he went to the office in them.

The day before she had been at her lover's house; she went there with a plan prepared, but it did not turn out as she wanted. She sat on his knee (thinking this necessary in view of the circumstances) and worked herself up into petulant gaiety; he was at once on the alert and asked what she wanted. She laughed and asked him not to buy her any more presents; she would rather buy them herself if only she had something to buy them with. He looked at her, and his hands fell to his sides. " Get up," he said, rose and walked up and down the room; then he counted out two hundred crowns and put them beside her handbag. Ah, she had purposely left her handbag on the table; she had thought it all out beforehand; why did he not understand, why did he leave it to her, when she said good-bye, to gather up the notes and cram them hastily and clumsily into her handbag? Why, at least, did he not turn away while she did so, why did he watch it all with a fixed, scrutinizing stare? Marie looked at the point of her needle with dry wide eyes; unconsciously she tore the silk, making a crooked hole in it with absent-minded thoroughness.

" That is just it, Marie," observed her husband with difficulty. " We haven't enough money."

" My handbag," said Marie irritably.

" What do you want? "

" Take . . . my handbag."

He opened the handbag; found the crumpled

bunch of notes just as she had stuffed them in the day before. " Is this yours ? " he gasped.

" Ours," said Marie.

Her husband stared dumbfounded at his wife's bent neck ; he did not know what to say. " Am I to put it by ? " he asked softly.

" If you like."

He shuffled about in his stockinged feet, trying to find a word of offence or tenderness ; finally without a word he went into the next room with the money. He was there a long time ; when he returned he found Marie still with bent head tearing the silk with her needle.

" Marie," he said softly, " wouldn't you like to come for a walk with me ? "

Marie shook her head.

Her husband lingered helplessly, it was impossible to talk about it *now*. . . . " Look here, Marie," he broke out at last with an air of relief, " suppose I go to a café now ? It's years now since I——"

" Go," whispered Marie.

He dressed, not knowing what to talk about ; but Marie did not stir, bent over the many-coloured silk, pretty, buxom, speechless. . . .

He dressed hurriedly as though he would take to flight ; at the door he hesitated again, stopped, and said vaguely : " You know,

Marie, if you like to go out—well—you can.
I may be out to supper."

Marie laid her head on the torn silk.
That day she was not granted the gift of
tears.

THE SHIRTS

HE wanted to think about other infinitely more important matters, but, do what he would, the unpleasant thought kept running through his mind : his housekeeper was robbing him. She had been with him so many years, and he had got quite out of the habit of keeping track of his personal belongings. There stood his linen-cupboard : in the morning he would open it and take a clean shirt from the top of the pile. From time to time, at irregular intervals, Mrs. Johanka would come and display before him a torn shirt, declaring that they were all in the same plight, and that master must buy new ones. Very good, master would then go out and buy half a dozen shirts at the first shop he came to, not, however, without a vague idea that he had gone through the same performance not very long before. It was the same with collars and ties, clothes and boots, soap, and the thousand and one other things which a man needs, even when he is a widower. Everything has to be renewed from time to time, but on an old man things all get somehow old and shabby at once, or goodness knows what happens to them; he was continually buying new things, only to be faced, when he opened his wardrobe, with a jumble of worn and faded garments made he could not tell when. But after all there was no need to bother about these things. Mrs. Johanka saw to everything.

Now, for the first time after all these years, it was borne in on him that he was being systematically robbed. It happened like this : he had received that morning an invitation to go to a banquet given by some society or other. For years he had been nowhere at all ; the narrow circle of his friends was so small that the unexpected invitation bewildered him altogether ; he was delighted beyond measure, but rather scared. First of all, he began searching to see if he had any shirt splendid enough ; he pulled them all out of the cupboard, but there was not one which was not frayed at the cuffs or round the collar. He called Johanka and asked her whether he had not some more presentable linen.

Mrs. Johanka gulped, was silent for a moment, and then declared sharply that master must certainly buy new ones ; it was useless for her to go on mending the old ones, they were regular cobwebs. He had, however, a vague impression that he had bought some not long before, but not being sure he was silent and at once began to put on his coat to go and buy them. But now he was once started on tidying up, he pulled some old papers out of his pockets to see if he should keep them or throw them away. Among them was the last bill for shirts, paid on such and such a date. Seven weeks ago. Seven weeks ago, half a dozen new shirts. That was his whole discovery.

He did not go and buy any others, but wandered about the room meditating. He looked back upon years and years of solitude. Since his wife's death Johanka had kept house for him, and never for a moment had he felt the least suspicion or distrust; but now an uneasy feeling came over him that he was being robbed all that time. He glanced about him; he could not say what was missing, but he suddenly perceived that the place was empty and desolate, and he tried to remember whether there used not to be more things about, a more intimate look, more of everything. . . . Full of dismay, he opened the chest in which lay memorials of his wife: dresses, linen. A few shabby articles were there, but all breath of the past was gone from them; heavens! the number of things which his wife had really left! What had become of them all?

He closed the chest and forced himself to

think of other things; for instance, the banquet that evening. But those past years returned insistently. They seemed now more desolate, bitter and miserable than when he was living through them; they appeared suddenly as if despoiled, and from them breathed an agony of desolation. Of course, at intervals he had been contented, lulled, as it were, to sleep; but now he was appalled to see the slumber of a lonely man whom strange hands robbed of even the pillow beneath his head; and he felt forlorn, suffering from a keen pain, greater than he had known since the day—the day when he returned from the funeral. He found himself grown old and weary, as one to whom life had been too cruel.

One thing, however, he could not make out: why should she steal my things? What would she do with them? Oh, I see, he remembered suddenly with a certain malicious satisfaction. That's what it is! She has a nephew somewhere whom she loves with the foolish love of an infatuated aunt; have I not had to listen to innumerable babblings about that flower of men? Let me see, not long ago she actually showed me his photo: curly hair, snub nose, and a particularly impertinent moustache; though she, for her part, wiped away tears of pride and emotion. So that's where all my things have strayed, he said to himself. He flew into a terrible rage at the thought; he ran to the kitchen and called out to Johanka something like, "You wretched old hag!" and then bolted away again, leaving her fearfully and tearfully rolling her old goggle sheep's eyes.

He did not speak to her again for the rest of that day; she sighed as though she had been insulted, and clattered things about whenever they came handy, not realizing in the least what the cause of the trouble was. In the afternoon he embarked on a complete overhauling of his cupboards and drawers; it was terrible; he remembered first one thing and then another which he had at some time possessed; various family heirlooms, which now seemed to him particularly precious. And now there was nothing left, nothing—not one thing left of it all. It was just as though there had been a great fire. He could have broken down and wept with rage and loneliness.

He was sitting in the midst of open drawers, out of breath, covered with dust, and holding in his hand the one solitary relic which was left —his father's purse, a bead bag with holes now at both ends. For how many years must she have been robbing him to have left nothing at all? He was almost beside himself with rage; if he had come across her at that moment he would have slapped her face. What shall I do with her? he said in emotion. Pack her off at once? Hand her over to the police? But who will cook for me to-morrow? I will go to a restaurant, he decided; but who will heat water and light the fire for me? With a supreme effort he drove these cares away. I will settle the matter to-morrow, he assured himself; something will turn up. The idea that I am dependent upon her! Nevertheless, the problem weighed on him more heavily than he would admit; only the consciousness of wrong suffered and the necessity of punishment kept up his courage.

When it grew dusk he pulled himself together so far as to go to the kitchen and say to Johanka carelessly, "You must go out somewhere or other," and then he gave her some complicated and lengthy errands of a somewhat irrelevant nature, which he said must be done at once, and which he had devised with no small trouble. Mrs. Johanka said nothing, but set about the business with the pained air of a martyr.

At last the door slammed behind her and he was left alone. With beating heart he stole to the kitchen, and then hesitated with his hand on the latch; he was seized with panic as he felt that he would never bring himself to the point of opening her cupboard: it seemed to him the act of a thief. But when he was already thinking of giving it up the thing came of itself; he opened the door and went in.

The kitchen literally shone with cleanliness. There stood Johanka's cupboard; but it was locked and no sign of a key. This discovery confirmed him in his purpose; he tried to force the cupboard with a kitchen knife, but he only hacked it about and did not succeed in opening it. He pulled out every drawer in search of a key, tried every key of his own; but at last, after half an hour of raging, he found that the cupboard was not locked at all, and could be opened with a button-hook.

Neatly arranged and ironed lay the linen on separate shelves. And just on the top were his six new shirts, still tied up with the blue ribbon from the shop. In a cardboard box was his wife's brooch with the dark amethyst; his father's mother-of-pearl cuff-links; his mother's portrait on ivory—goodness, had she a use even for that? He pulled everything out of the cupboard: he found his socks and collars, a box of soap, tooth-brushes, an old silk waist-coat, pillow-cases, an old officer's pistol, and a smoke-stained and quite useless amber mouthpiece. These were indeed portions of his wardrobe; the greater part had evidently been made over long ago to the curly-headed nephew. The heat of passion subsided, but there remained the reproachful distress. So this is how it is. . . . Johanka, Johanka, how have I deserved this from you?

One by one he removed his things to his own room and spread them out on the table; they formed an imposing exhibition of every imaginable article. Those which were Johanka's property he threw back into the cupboard in the kitchen; he even wanted to put them neatly in order, but after some attempts he retreated helplessly, leaving the cupboard gaping open as if after a robbery. And then he began to be afraid that Johanka would return, and that he would have to talk to her seriously. . . . The idea disgusted him so much that he began to dress hurriedly. To-morrow I will take her to task, he said to himself; to-day it will be enough for her to realize that I have found out. He picked up one of the new shirts, which was as stiff as paper, so that with all his efforts he could not manage to fasten his stiff collar. And Johanka might come back at any moment.

He dived quickly into his old shirt, regardless of the fact that it was torn, and no sooner was he dressed than he slunk out like a thief, and for an hour loitered about the streets in the rain until it was time to go to the banquet. At the gathering he felt lonely; he tried to fall into intimate talk with old acquaintances; but in some way, he did not know how, the years had come between him and other people; just imagine it, we can hardly understand each other. But he had no grudge against anyone; he stood apart and smiled, dazzled by the glare of lights and the noise and movement . . . until for some unknown reason he was seized with fresh alarm—just think what I must look like ! There are threads hanging from my shirt, a stain on my dress coat, and as for my boots, bless me ! He wished he could sink into the ground, and looked round for a hiding-place, but on every side there shone brilliant shirt-fronts—where could he slip away unnoticed ? He was afraid to take a step towards the door lest every glance should suddenly be turned upon him. He perspired with embarrassment; he pretended to be standing motionless, but all the time he was shuffling with his feet so as to reach the door by inches, without being perceived. As ill-luck would have it an old acquaintance, a fellow-student of his at the High School, accosted him, which added to his embarrassment. He answered him confusedly, and very nearly offended him; he breathed a sigh of relief when he was once more alone, and measured his distance from the door. At length he escaped and fled home; it was not yet midnight.

On the way Johanka came into his mind

again. His brain became active with rapid walking, and he planned in his mind what he should say to her. With unaccustomed ease, long, forceful, dignified phrases strung themselves together : a lengthy discourse of severe condemnation and ultimate mercy. Yes, mercy ; because in the end he would forgive her. He would not turn her into the street. Johanka would weep and implore, then promise to mend her ways ; he would listen in silence, unmoved, and at last would say to her solemnly : " Johanka, I will give you a chance to make amends for your ingratitude ; be honest and loyal, I ask no more of you. I am an old man and do not wish to be cruel."

He was so excited that before he realized it he found himself at home and had unlocked the door. A light was burning in Johanka's room. He just peeped through the curtain into the kitchen ; good gracious, what was that ? Johanka, her face flushed and swollen with weeping, was rushing about the kitchen and throwing her things into a trunk. He was terribly alarmed. Why the trunk ? He crept to his room on tiptoe, confused, oppressed, and quite bewildered. Was Johanka going away ?

There in front of him on the table lay all the things she had stolen from him. He fingered them, but felt not the smallest pleasure at their recovery. I see, he said to himself, Johanka has discovered that I have found her guilty of thieving and expects to be sent off at once—that is why she is packing up. Very well, I will leave her with that idea—until to-morrow ; that will be sufficient punishment for her ; yes, I will talk to her in the morning. But perhaps—perhaps, even now she will come and ask my pardon. She will burst into tears before me, fall on her knees and that sort of thing. That will do, Johanka, I don't want to be harsh ; you can stay.

He sat down in his evening clothes to await developments. There was silence, unbroken silence in the house ; he heard every step of Johanka's in the kitchen, heard the angry slamming of a trunk lid, then again calm. What was that ? He sprang up in alarm and listened : a prolonged, terrible howl, as of some creature not human ; then it trailed off into a series of hysterical sobs ; there followed the sound of knees sinking heavily to the floor, and subdued moaning. Johanka was weeping. He had certainly been prepared for something, but this was unexpected. With beating heart he stood and listened to what was going on in the kitchen. Nothing, only weeping. Presently Johanka will come to herself and ask for forgiveness.

He paced the room in order to recover his

firmness, but still Johanka did not come. At intervals he stopped and listened; her wailing changed into a monotonous series of unabated howls. This dreadful despair was distressing to him. I will go to her, he resolved, and just say: "Now, let this be a lesson to you, Johanka, and stop crying. I will forget all about it, but be honest in future."

Suddenly a violent rush, the door burst open, and there stood Johanka on the threshold, howling; it was dreadful to see her face so swollen with weeping.

"Johanka," he gasped.

"Have—I—deserved this?" broke from Johanka. "Nice thanks this—as if I were a thief—such a shame!"

"But, Johanka," he cried alarmed, "but you have taken my things—all these, do you see? Did you take them or not?"

But Johanka did not hear. "What I have to put up with—such a shame—searching in my cupboard—as if—I was—some pilfering gipsy. To shame me so, me, indeed—you shouldn't have done it, sir—no right to—insult me—never—not to my dying day—would I have expected the like. Am I a thief indeed? I—I a thief, indeed?" She shrieked in passionate distress. "Am I really a thief? I, indeed, considering my family! That—that I never did expect—never deserved such a thing!"

"But, Johanka," he said, somewhat damped, "just have some sense. How did these things get into your cupboard? Is this yours or mine? Say, my good woman, is this yours?"

"I don't want to hear anything," sobbed Johanka. "Good Lord, what a shame! Just as if—I was a gipsy—search my cupboard!—but this instant," she cried, fearfully excited, "this instant I'll be off. I shall not stop here, till the morning. No—no."

"But look here," he protested in alarm, "I don't want to turn you out. You will stay on, Johanka. As for what has happened, well, heaven save us from anything worse. I have not yet said a word to you about it. So stop crying."

"Engage someone else," said Johanka, choking with tears. "I shall not stay here even till to-morrow morning. As if one were—a dog—to put up with anything—I won't," she ejaculated desperately, "not if you paid me thousands. I would rather spend the night on the pavement."

"But why, Johanka," he argued helplessly. "Have I hurt your feelings, then? But still you cannot deny——"

"No, not hurt my feelings," cried Johanka in a still more wounded tone. "It is not hurting my feelings—searching my cupboard —as if I were a thief. That is nothing at all—

that I have to put up with—no one ever did such a thing to me—such a shame. I am not —just a tramp," she shrieked with a convulsive burst of tears and rushed out, slamming the door.

He was immensely perplexed. Instead of repentance, all this scene. What does it mean? She steals like a jackdaw, no doubt of that, and feels insulted because I know about it; not ashamed of being a thief, but terribly hurt in her sensitiveness when put down as one. Is the woman out of her mind?

But gradually he felt more and more sorry for her. You see, he said to himself, everyone has his weak spot, but you never offend him more than by remarking on it. Ah, what an unbounded moral sensitiveness man harbours even amid his faults! How painfully and tenderly susceptible even in his misdeeds! Just put your finger on his secret vice and you hear nothing but a cry of pain and indignation in reply. Do you not see that in judging the offender you are judging the offended?

From the kitchen came the sound of weeping stifled by a feather bed. He wanted to go in, but the door was locked; he stood there trying to reason with her, upbraided her, and then attempted to soothe her; but all the reply he met with was more violent and noisy sobbing. He went back to his room oppressed with helpless pity. There on the table lay the stolen articles: fine new shirts, a quantity of linen, mementos, and what not. He caressed them with his finger, but in the touch there was something sad and forlorn.

THE INSULT

VOJTECH was fast asleep (it was a November night, when bed is a comfortable place to be in) when there came a sudden knocking on his window with a stick. The sleeper took one moment more to finish his dream, in which the knocking played a decisive but somewhat confused part, and awoke. There! again, and again! The sleeper pulled the bed-clothes over his ears and determined not to hear anything. The stick, however, renewed its drumming on the glass in a violent and peremptory manner. Vojtech jumped out of bed, opened the window, and saw on the pavement below a man with his collar turned up.

"What do you want here?" he cried, letting his voice betray his angry annoyance.

"Make me a cup of tea," replied the voice below hoarsely.

The sleeper recognized his brother, and at last woke up. The pitiless cold of the night gripped his chest. "Wait a minute," he flung down, turned on the light and began to dress hurriedly. It was only while he was dressing that it occurred to him that he had not spoken to his brother for two years; they had quarrelled about a legacy. He suddenly fell to wondering so much about his coming that he forgot to put on his shoes. He sat there, shoe in hand, shaking his head. Why had he come? Obviously, something had happened to him, he realized at last, and threw on his clothes and rushed to the window again. His brother was not down there any more, he was walking away and had already got as far as the corner of the street. Perhaps he had found the waiting too long. Vojtech dashed out into the passage, opened the front door and ran after him.

His brother was going off at a brisk pace without looking round. "Karel," called Vojtech as he ran; he was sure that his brother heard him, but that he did not want to stop or even slacken his pace. He started off after him at a run, calling excitedly: "Karel, what are you doing, Karel? . . . I say, stop a minute, do!"

Karel strode on quickly. Shivering with cold, half-dressed, bewildered, Vojtech stopped. Now for the first time he felt that it was raining. Karel went straight on, turned suddenly, and came back just as quickly towards his brother. For a moment Vojtech could not for the life of him think what to say to his brother. For two years they had not been on speaking terms. He was an obstinate fellow. Now he stood there with flashing eyes, biting his lips.

"Then you won't give me a cup of tea?" grumbled Karel, sullen and angry.

"Yes, of course, I will, with pleasure," gasped Vojtech, much relieved. "I was only just a minute. . . . Come along quickly, I'll make you some at once."

"At last," snapped Karel bitterly.

"Why, good heavens!" Vojtech interrupted him eagerly, "in any case. . . . You could have come long ago. In half a minute . . . anything you want—if you'd like something to eat—I'll be only too glad—just say."

"Thanks, just a cup of tea."

"I've got some bacon from Moravia, how about that? Or an egg . . . I haven't the least idea what the time is. It's ages since we saw each other, isn't it, Karel? Would you like some wine?"

"No."

"All right, just say. Anything you like. . . . Look out, there are steps here."

"I know."

At last Vojtech got him home. He laughed, chattered, offered all kinds of things, and made

excuses—" An old bachelor, you know "—
hunted out smoking tackle and cleared a chair
or two, hardly noticing that he was doing all
the talking himself. But all the time the
vigilant, restless, inquisitive thought remained
with him : something must have happened to
his brother.

Karel sat frowning and lost in thought.
There was an oppressive silence. " Has
anything happened ? " Vojtech burst out.

" No."

Vojtech shook his head, puzzled. He did
not recognize his brother like this. He was
reeking of wine and women. And yet he was a
married man ; he had a young wife, gentle as
a lamb, a meek, pretty creature ; for years
he had stayed quietly at home enjoying efficient
control of domestic affairs, a paragon of life
economy ; rather austere, methodical, precise,
and with an inordinately high opinion of
himself. Once he had been very ill, and since
that time he ran his life on extremely hygienic
and orderly lines, as if life had a value in itself
and was to be bought back day by day through
regular habits and self-control. And now he
was sitting there, his brows knit in frowning
sobriety, like a man just awakened after a night
of dissipation ; there he sat with an indescrib-
able expression on his face, tense, and as if
with difficulty biting back evil words. It was

obvious that something terrible was going on within him.

It was three o'clock in the morning. Vojtech clapped his hand to his forehead suddenly. " Good heavens, the tea ! " he remembered with womanly concern, and hurried off to the kitchen. It was bitterly cold. He wrapped himself up in a shawl like an old woman and heated the water over the blue flame of the spirit lamp, quite glad to be doing something mechanical. He set out cups and saucers and sugar, comforted by the intimate clinking of the things ; he could only see into the other room through the crack of the door, and there stood his brother at the open window, as if he were listening to the roar of the Vltava's weir, an all-pervading and steady voice which like a veil obscured the cold patter of the rain.

" Aren't you cold ? " asked Vojtech anxiously.

" No."

Vojtech stood at the door in melancholy constraint. Here on the one side a quiet, dark, little den, just cheered by the pleasant hissing of the lamp ; a dear, cosy, little den, a draught of something warm, the joy of being at home, the delight of giving hospitality ; on the other side a wide open window filled with the majestic voice of river and darkness, as though perhaps the night itself were rolling over the Vltava's weir to make it roar so ; and at the window a tall man standing erect, strangely unfamiliar, strangely excited : your own brother whom you do not recognize. Vojtech stood on the threshold as on the border of two worlds : his own intimate world and his brother's strange one, which was somehow unusually grand and terrible at that moment. He knew that some secret was to be revealed to him, that his brother had come to tell him something supremely important; he was afraid of this, scared outright, as he listened with alert, microscopic attention to the hissing of the lamp and the broad murmur of the river.

With motherly care Vojtech set the steaming, ruddy tea on the table and asked : " I say, wouldn't you like something to eat ? " In a minute he was back with bacon and biscuits, pressing him to eat and bustling about; he grew femininely tender, like a kindly solicitous aunt. Karel merely sipped at his tea and then, it seemed, forgot his thirst. " You see——" he began and stopped. He sat there with his face buried in his hands and thought no more of what he had wanted to say.

All at once he straightened up. " Listen, Vojto," he began, " I just wanted to say— that was a stupid business, our quarrel. Please don't think that the money mattered to me. Perhaps you thought it did. It makes no difference to me, but it's not true. It was only a question of form, and then . . . I don't care that about money." he cried excitedly snapping his fingers. "Not that much. Nor about anything. I shall get on without anything at all."

Vojtech melted completely. Touched beyond measure, he broke into assurances that for long he had not given it a thought, that they had both been to blame, and so on. . . . Karel did not heed him. "All right, that's enough," he said, "I don't want to talk about that. It's quite beside the point. I only wanted—to ask you," the words fell from his lips hesitatingly, "to do something for me. Let my wife know that I have left the office."

"But why, why——" cried Vojtech in amazement. "Do you mean you're not going back to her?"

"I don't want to yet, d'you understand? and perhaps not at all—that is quite irrelevant. Anyway she can go back to her people if she feels lonely. I only want not to be disturbed. There's something I have got to start, I have a kind of plan—but for the present the details don't matter. The main thing is that I must be by myself, d'you understand?"

"I don't understand at all. What's wrong with the office?"

"Nothing, some nonsense or other. It's all the same to me what has happened or is going to happen there. You don't think that is troubling me at all, do you ? "

" What is troubling you then ? "

" Nothing at all. That is quite beside the point. I don't think about it any more now. On the contrary, I'm glad of it, very glad. Vojto," turning to him confidentially all at once, " now please tell me the truth quite honestly. Do you think I am cut out for an official ? Tell me now, do you ? "

" I—d—don't know," stammered Vojtech.

" I mean to say, if you know me a little from former days, do you think that can be enough for me ? Do you think I could be satisfied with it ? That I haven't the right or—don't need to live a quite different life ? Do you really think that ? "

" No, I don't think so," said Vojtech reluctantly and unconvinced, trying to take in with a single glance the whole of his brother's regular, transparently temperate life ; a life which he had sometimes envied him ; a life in which he had never taken a close interest.

" Perhaps it looked like that," continued Karel reflectively. "Or perhaps it was slumbering in me. You see, Vojto, I never even knew, myself, but now I know quite well."

" What do you mean ? "

" Oh, what does it matter ? " Karel brushed the subject aside and fell into thought.

Vojtech waited a moment. "Look here, Karel," he began, "something has happened to you; you are angry or hurt—and you are letting your imagination run away with you. Tell me first what has happened to you. Perhaps it can be put right. Certainly it can. And as for your not going back to your wife and the office, that is absolute nonsense. You can't really be serious and—are you listening?"

Karel stood up and laughed. "That'll do," he said, and began walking about the room. Now for the first time he looked about him, stopped in front of pictures, and noticed the things standing about. "Poor old Vojto," he jeered, "so this is where you live? And all alone? And you have room enough here to live your whole life? your whole life? Look here, supposing you got married. Married like me! Suppose you had a nice little wife. Someone to look after you as if you were a wilful child. To make you her little boy because she is afraid of childbirth and has no children. Think if you had a nest of pillows— like me! Why, man, you don't know what happiness is!"

"You are not fair to your wife," objected Vojtech gently.

"Of course I am unfair to her," retorted Karel, "and more than that: she bores me,

I've had enough of her. You must tell her that, but tell her too that I know I wrong her. Tell her that she has been the model of an official's wife. Oh God! it's an absolute crime. Think of it, she has been waiting for me all the evening! All the evening she has been keeping up the fire, looking at the thermometer, laying the table and waiting; consider, she doesn't suspect anything yet! Still waiting even now, getting alarmed, sitting on the bed, unable to make it out. . . . Until in the morning you come to her and say, ' Madam, your husband has gone off.' "

" I shall not tell her that ! "

" You will say : He has gone off because he is disgusted with himself; he is awfully bored with all he knows of himself. Just think, he has just discovered in himself a soul which he never knew before, a rather worse soul, violent, strange, and he wants to make a fresh start with it. He cannot sleep with you any longer because your husband was a quite different person; he was a homely fool who drank warmed beer and was loved by you. Tell her that, Vojto, you understand? Say to her, Madam, he hates warmed beer, he even hates you, for yesterday he drank iced and fiery wine and was unfaithful to you; he has found another sort of woman for himself and is going to her—Ah, man." Karel dropped suddenly from dramatic rhetoric to eager under-tones, " It's awful for that poor girl, if you could see her wretchedness. Christ ! what a life ! Her feet were frozen through like ice, so that they simply couldn't be warmed. I must go back to her because of her wretchedness. If you could see the way she lives ! It can't be remedied by giving her money ; you see, she drinks it all away, but somebody ought to be with her——"

" Karel ! " said Vojtech hoarsely.

" Wait a bit and don't talk," Karel defended himself. " It isn't only that. That is after all really beside the point. At first I did not even think of women. But really, Vojto, can a man go back to his pillows and lambrequins when he has seen such misery ? You know, of course, what it's like at home ; I could smother myself in it all for shame and disgust. That, of course, my wife couldn't understand. Oh, I know she is good and sweet ; you needn't speak about that anyway. I did not mean to begin about it at all ; it is only a detail and it really only began after that."

" After what ? "

" After I had decided. Wait, you don't know anything about it yet. It all began quite differently. It began . . . while I was still in the office. To put it shortly—well, there was a row in the office—and I," Karel brought his fist down on the table in violent anger, " I was in the right, and there's an end of it."

" What was the row about ? " inquired Vojtech attentively.

" Oh, nothing, some nonsense. It really isn't worth mentioning at all. It was the last straw, you know. But you feel trampled on and simply can't defend yourself. Just as if you were a rag. So I stayed on in the office and looked through documents and books, and it appeared that I was quite clearly in the right ; someone else had made a blunder, but who ? It's strange that that's all the same to me now ; but at the time I writhed like a worm and made up my mind to kill myself."

" Karel ! " cried Vojtech.

" You—you be quiet," Karel commanded drunkenly, stretching out a trembling finger towards him, " you are like that, too. All the evening I've been wandering about the streets ; I didn't want to go home. I just let myself drift. I was tired and only wanted to go and get drunk. I found a drinking-shop, you know, a low-down sort of den ; I had never seen anything like it : music and women and so much squalor—awful. I've forgotten now who else was sitting there with me ; one girl had awfully sore fingers, losing her nails ; is that a symptom of disease, do you know ? "

" Why do you ask ? "

" Because she kept on drinking from my glass—I couldn't prevent her; but it doesn't matter now. Then there was one man, I was talking to him the whole evening; I don't know who he was. I got the idea that they'd all come there as I had, guests and women, the whole lot of them; perhaps they wanted to kill themselves, too, because they were unhappy, and that's why they were there. I felt that I had something in common with them, but in a different and deeper sense than, say, with my colleagues at the office: that somehow I must suddenly go selling matches and be filthy and old in the place of that matchseller; or that I, too, must lose my nails painfully, that I must become a prostitute or go thieving at night, just as they do. Think of this, Vojto: I got the idea that while I was sitting there the end of the world was happening outside and nothing was left but that drinking-shop and the people in it; harlots, women playing the harp, thieves, drunkards and diseased people; and this was now humanity. There were no more churches or palaces, no more philosophy or art, glory or states, but only that score of outcasts. Can you imagine that ? "

" Just go on with your story."

" No, nothing more. I just wondered what I should do in such circumstances. What should I do, for instance, with my documents, my title and worldly wisdom? Why, man, with all that I could not cheer up a single one of them, or give them a vivid idea of human virtue or degradation. There would be no example or image of anything; if I were to play the harp or to cry, it would be a hundred times better; do you understand?"

"Yes."

"You know, Vojto, that's why I came to you, because you were sure to understand. For me it threw a light on my whole life. The life I had been living was useless. It had been no good even to me myself. Perhaps it was of some use, possibly to the state; but the state is only something formal—the state is for example, the duty on wine; but it isn't wine, or a tavern, or a squalid drunkard, or a diseased barmaid; these are facts, d'you understand? A man must go by facts and not merely lay down rules—— Anyway, I was suddenly disgusted with it. You know, Vojto, an official is a man who obeys and makes others obey, and that's all he does; and the higher officials, such as I was, don't know at all whether people are ill, or what they're like. You've got to see disease, misery and filth, otherwise you can't know. But when you have merely seen and observed them carefully, and perhaps done nothing more, even so you do by this very fact render a great service to humanity; it makes you miserable, drives you mad, makes you ill, and that is a great deal, far more than when you sit healthy and happy among your cushions. That's how it is."

At that moment it was infinitely pleasant to Vojtech to listen. Snugly wrapped up, his knees hunched up to his chin, huddled in his rug, he sat like a child, charmed as much by the speaker's voice and gestures as by his words. "Go on. More," he said.

"More," said Karel meditatively, "what more was there? When I had decided never to go back to the office I suddenly felt an immense relief. I didn't feel any longer that I wanted to kill myself. On the contrary, I saw now that I was just beginning, that this was the starting-point of a new life. That, I can tell you, is a tremendous sensation; I had never experienced anything so wonderful. I wandered about the town again, not thinking of what I was going to do, but round about everywhere; and even behind the walls of the houses I could feel something absolutely new. And just because it was all so wonderful, I knew that I had arrived at something splendid and true. You know, Vojto, inspiration is the greatest happiness of all. It's a thing that can't be expressed in words, but it is as if you were talking with God, or as if the whole world, earth and stars and all humanity, yes, even past generations, were all thinking your own thoughts with you. It is a happiness like that. Then I came across that girl and she spoke to me. I went to find out whether that amazing, that more than earthly beauty could survive even in such—such horror. And Vojto, would you believe it, I felt freer and freer. When I saw her wretchedness I felt as if I were growing wings. If now I were to see all the misery and horror in the whole world, I should only be happier and more sure within myself. I must still know infinitely more, because that makes one free. Are you asleep?"

"No, I'm not asleep.'

"The more misery one sees, the more one has in common with the world. I have discovered the spirit of fellowship: it is not sympathy at all, it is enlightenment and ecstasy; it is not pity but enthusiasm. You, yourself——" he pronounced this oration standing upright with arm outstretched; his intoxication, previously overcome by excitement, mastered him more and more powerfully—"you yourself then see every pain and discover every wretchedness and disease and feel them to be your own. You are poor and wretched, a thief and a harlot, a drunkard, a thing past hope; you are that which you see. And you long only to bear all misery and every sickness, to take all degradation upon yourself ; you yearn and crave to be satisfied. You will not give alms to the poor, because you will not right the old wrong ; but you will be poor yourself, you must be as poor as they if you would put it right. You must be diseased, drunken, hunted, insulted, mud-bespattered, rejected of men. You must reach the supreme point. You must reach that utterly supreme point. You know enough, quite enough ; forget it all ; you must learn now. But, Vojto," he turned to him suddenly with unusual kindliness, " you must be wanting to sleep."

"No, really not," Vojtech assured him eagerly.

"Go and lie down, I've something I must write. Do go to sleep ; you would only disturb me."

" No, Karel," pleaded Vojtech, " I shan't go to sleep. Write if you want to ; I shall just lie still so as not to disturb you ; but afterwards I have something to say to you."

" All right, but do go to sleep," repeated Karel, seating himself at the table and burying his head in his hands.

Quietly stretched out in bed Vojtech thought over what he would say to his brother. He was perplexed and full of pity ; he tried to find some particularly affectionate words which should be like a beaming glance. Considerate words like those we use to someone ill. Something by which he could comfort him and make it up to him.

With half-closed eyes he watched his brother, bent over the table as if he were studying. He always learned with difficulty and very stubbornly. He used to have passionate cravings which he overcame by studying. He was so ambitious and headlong. A young drunkard, he had one day entirely given up drinking because he had made up his mind to. Or he would decide to get up at five o'clock in the morning. He got up and studied, Vojtech meanwhile snored in his lair, luxurious and warmth-loving as a cat. " Vojto, Vojto, get up, it's seven o'clock already." No sound from Vojtech ; as if he had not heard ; but all the time he hears the scratching of pen on paper and is snugly conscious of a living creature so near him. For nothing in the world would he open his eyes. He wants to finish his dream ; but really it is not a dream (smiled Vojtech to himself), it actually happened when I was in about the fourth form : some fellows in the seventh form, fellow-students of Karel's, took me to a tavern, wait a minute, there was Kislingr and Dostálek—he's dead now. . . . Then Vojtech hears a woman singing to the harp, " And I am Esmeralda, faithful daughter of the

South, Esmeralda, Esmeralda———" He likes it, but he is afraid that they will turn him out; he makes himself as small as he can, so that nobody shall see him. He hides behind the table and only looks at the girl who carries round the wine. Now with arms uplifted she smoothes her hair and sings; now she speaks to one of them, bending towards his face, kneeling with one knee on a chair, a red garter below the other knee; Vojtech does not know where to turn his eyes, he is ashamed of them, he is jealous, and he watches—— And now, great heavens! she sees me! She goes straight to him, swaying a little; she leans right across the table, looking at him from very close with her strange, shining pupils, humming a little song about love, and quietly, lovingly, she laughs; Vojtech feels her damp breath on his lips, and could almost cry with shame and love. He wants to speak, but he does not know what to say; she, too, does not know, and so she only murmurs the little song about love and looks into his eyes with her close, bright gaze. What did she want of me? Why did she not speak? Why, the boys are not here any more, but here sits Karel, writing at his deed-folio and saying: " Now you must study." But Vojtech pretends not to hear; study as much as you like, he thinks, but let me sleep now.

When Vojtech woke it was broad day ; he was surprised to find himself in bed half-dressed; then he remembered a little and looked for Karel. Karel was lying on the couch asleep. His face looked worn and painfully tired, and he looked older. Then Vojtech, quietly, so as not to wake him, looked for what he had written the night before. He found a letter in a sealed envelope, tore it open and read :

SIR,

On account of illness I beg to tender my resignation and I request that I may be granted discharge without pension.

N.N., ex-counsellor.

Vojtech shook his head and searched further. In the waste-paper basket were some crumpled and much corrected and torn sheets ; he smoothed them out and read :

DEAR SIR,

Kindly compare the deed which was taken from me yesterday with the supplement B3 in the file M-XXIII., with the Minister's dictation in the above-mentioned file and with the copy of the letter of the 17th September in the same, which prove that I am not to blame for the mistaken decision, but that I got faulty material from the protocol. You will see for yourself, in spite of your youth, that the Minister was unjust to me—

Here was the letter, torn and crumpled in evident anger. A further sheet ought from appearances to contain the beginning of a treatise; there was only:

If you wish to become a philosopher, you must—

But this sheet, too, was crumpled and torn, perhaps after the long wakeful hours.

Vojtech carefully put together the pathetic papers and with a heart aching with pity, looked at his sleeping brother. You could see that he was already grey at the temples, swollen under the eyes, and he seemed ill. Vojtech watched him with careful attention; then he quietly finished dressing, shut the door after him, and hurried to his brother's office.

He had acquaintances there, and it was easy for him to find out what had happened the previous day. In the afternoon the Minister had burst into the department quite beside himself with rage. "It is disgraceful," he bellowed from the doorway, "whoever did it is either a fool or a dishonourable man." It is true that he did not say it in exactly those words, but he implied something still worse. "And who is supposed to have done this?" he cried, waving a draft. Everybody was trembling with apprehension; then Karel said, " That is my draft," and would have defended himself. " Silence, sir ! " cried the Minister, and tore up the draft and threw it on to the desk of the youngest clerk in the department, his favourite. " Put that right, sir ! " And slammed the door behind him. Everyone remained as if stunned. Karel, pale, and to all appearances moving like an automaton, shut his desk and went out without a word. At five o'clock he returned and worked while everyone went home. None of them, indeed, believed that he had committed any blunder ; but he did not want to talk to anyone. Then Vojtech, almost by force, penetrated to the Minister, a terrible and explosive man ; after half an hour he appeared in the doorway, flushed, exhausted, but with the light of victory in his eyes : the Minister himself conducted him as far as the door in order to shake him once again by the hand. Vojtech flew home ; he found Karel sitting despondently on the sofa, worn out with fatigue and wrapped in a circle of thought.

" Karel ! " he announced triumphantly, " you're to go to the Minister."

" I'm not going," said Karel absent-mindedly.

" Yes, you are, because—because he wants to apologize to you ; that is, he begs you to come in order that he may express his regret and confidence. And his regard." Vojtech quickly recalled the words which he had prepared beforehand.

"Why did you go there?" Karel spoke heavily. "It's no good anyway, I don't want to and—I want to be left alone, Vojto. It's better for me so. Please leave me now. I've something immensely more important to think of now. . . ."

There was a painful silence. Vojtech bit his nails in despair. "And what are you going to do now? Tell me that," he said at last.

"I don't know," said Karel reluctantly, and began to pace about the room.

Somebody rang. It was a chauffeur. "The Minister has sent his car for the counsellor," he announced in the doorway.

Karel gave a start; he searched his brother's eyes suspiciously to see if he were by any chance playing a trick on him; he saw, however, only naïve surprise.

He was overcome now by an absurd feeling, the emotion which overcomes one suddenly at some kind little attention. Tears rose to his eyes; he blushed, and turned to the window. Right in front of the window shone the polished fittings of a splendid car.

"Well," he said hesitatingly, "I will go."

He suddenly began to hurry very much; and Vojtech helped him with such elaborate and confused haste that they had hardly time to say good-bye.

When Vojtech stepped to the window the street was already empty; and because he felt desolate and homesick, he went to announce to Karel's wife that her husband was coming back to her.

THE TRIBUNAL

THE court-martial was sitting in a small station building. A man had been brought in, arrested in the very act of murdering a wounded man. He was still young, sallow, bathed in a sweat of terror; from his lips, bruised from a rifle butt, dripped blood, which he was smearing over his face with horribly stained hands, lacerated to the bone. He was a sickeningly hideous object; shivering all over, dirty, abject, and wretched below all human level.

The presiding officer was putting questions to him. The man did not reply. He did not even state his name. He threw glances of panic and bitter hatred on every side. Then the soldiers gave their evidence noisily, with spiteful zeal. The case was manifestly clear; he had finished off a wounded soldier and was in the act of pulling off his wristlet watch. The presiding officer drummed with his fingers on the desk where, only the day before, a Morse apparatus had been tapping: no further questioning was needed. "In accordance with martial law," he said at length, " I condemn this man to be shot. Take him away." The man did not understand a single word; unresisting, he let himself be removed snuffling, and wiped his lips with blood-smeared hands. The trial was over.

The presiding officer unbuckled his sword and went to take a breath of air in front of the little railway station. It was a moonlight night. Everything was as if crystallized in marble light. The white road, white trees, shining meadows stretching as far as the eye could reach. Transparent whiteness, crystalline yearning, measureless and aching tension as far as one could see. Beyond the range of vision, an aching and luminous silence. A shining, lifeless, icily calm night. Not even a star, no friendly sign; there is nothing, nothing but this frigid glare.

The officer bowed his head. From the railway station waiting-room sounded the snoring of sleeping soldiers. The very darkness protects itself by the healthy, hearty snores against the splendour of the moonlight night; it gives voice to overcome its own apprehensions. But somewhere in the background beyond the rails was a hut, where the condemned man was confined, and where were gloom and silence; only a chink admitted the dread moonlight.

How the sweat of anguish poured from him ! Now the officer remembered that he had never shifted his gaze from his forehead. All at once a drop of sweat broke out and flowed quickly down the forehead ; another and again another. As if the whole forehead were shedding tears.

Alas, had everything become lifeless under that chill hoar-frost of light ? Not a beast stirring, not a mole making tracks across the grass, not the pipe of a bird to show that it lived ? Are things but phantoms, with only an unearthly radiance and this lonely man shivering in the gleaming frost ?

Suddenly a vast, mighty voice made itself heard, as if the moonlight spoke " There is no law."

The officer stiffened. Who says, who dares to say there is no law ? Listen, all of us here stand before the law ; we are surrounded by law as by the bounds of the horizon. How could we do anything unless we were compelled ? How could I keep my thirty soldiers together or command them if there were no law ? Whither could I go now if there were no law ? There would be no justice ; man himself could not exist without law ; nothing could exist, and the world would crumble away.

The calm voice replied, speaking through the moonlight, " There is no justice."

What, protested the exasperated officer, how

dare you say there is no justice! I condemned him because he killed a wounded man; I acted in the name of the law. And if there were no law, I should have acted according to my conscience, and killed him on the spot. I would have split his head open with my pistol and my conscience would have been clear.

Then spoke the infinite voice: " There is no conscience ! "

The president of the count-martial stood erect to oppose this terrible voice. Look on the platform, he retorted passionately, three soldiers lie there slain. Three young men who were alive this morning. This morning they laughed and talked jokingly in their rough, jolly voices. You will be killed with grief and rage, infuriated and maddened ; in the name of righteousness and conscience you will strike and judge in wrath and fury ; and were you God Himself you could do no other, no other than to agree with the man.

The voice which spoke through the moonlight was silent. The solitary man looked straight towards the sky, which seemed like a vast, white dome filled with frozen light. Then spoke the voice : " There is no God." The man shuddered and was aghast. Surely now the smallest blade of grass, the dust on the road, the white stone, the drops of criminal blood now drying on the threshold will raise themselves at once towards heaven and cry out in protest: they will be His champions and ardently bear witness to Him—at least they will make some sound, at least they will show their horror! Silence, deadly silence; only one of the slumbering soldiers behind there, talking in his sleep. Nothing stirs. The boundless landscape is tense with the silence of the universe.

But what of me, asked the man in terror, why does no voice sound from me in reply? No sign granted to me? Nothing, no one to aid me.

Someone murmured among the soldiers, someone awoke heavily; midnight and change of guard; grunting, coughing, and with his straps clicking a soldier came on guard.

The officer started and turned round; the blinking light of a lantern, warm, greasy, friendly, greeted him in the passage, and he took it from its place to serve him as a companion and went out on the platform. By the rail were three corpses: three murdered soldiers. Nothing more. The moonlight draped them in an icy veil of weird, remote aloofness.

Before the wooden gates of a shed a soldier was patrolling. Ten paces, ten paces; a bayonet edge gleamed whenever he turned. The sand of the platform, the white framework of the square shed, all white, dazzling, unearthly spectral. There is nothing. Absolutely nothing. Only the universe.

The officer made his way slowly to the room where he dispensed justice, threw himself on the sofa and set the wretched little railway lamp at the sofa's head ; the little oil flame trembled, shrinking into itself for warmth, and the man on the sofa kept his gaze fixed upon it, until his eyes filled with tears, until exhausted with grief and weariness he fell asleep.

THE BULLY

THE counting-house, with its electric lamps lighting it like an operating theatre rumbled and shook with the roar of the factory, but as the clock was on the stroke of six, the clerks were leaving their stools and washing their hands. The house-phone sounded, the cashier lifted the receiver and heard one word: "Bliss." Replacing the receiver, he winked at a young man, who, leaning on the office safe and bright with golden dentistry, chatted with a couple of typists. The young man showed all his teeth, threw away his cigarette, and went out.

Taking three stairs in a stride he ran up to the first floor. In the ante-room, nobody. Bliss stood a moment, shifting from one foot to the other, coughed, and passed through the double door into Pelican's private office. Beside Pelican's table he saw the Work's Manager, standing as a soldier stands making his report.

"I beg your pardon," Bliss purred quickly and stepped back.

"Stay," shot the command after him. The Works Manager with a spasmodic contraction, his nerves strained by the mere effort of sustained attention, twitched one side of his face. Pelican was writing. Through one corner of his mouth he spoke abruptly, while at the other was a cigar at which he bit. Suddenly he threw down the pen and said: "To-morrow announce a lock-out."

"That means a strike," observed the manager gloomily.

Pelican shrugged his shoulders.

The manager's face twitched nervously; evidently he had much on his mind. Meanwhile, Bliss discreetly looked out of the window, as if trying to give the impression that in reality he was not there. He knew well all that was at stake. For a year now he had closely watched Pelican's struggle for life. German competition had day by day been killing this huge roaring factory which to-morrow would perhaps be silenced for good. Do what they would, the Germans were thirty per cent cheaper. A year ago Pelican had extended the plant and sunk capital on a grotesquely large scale in new machinery for the purpose of cheapening output. He had purchased new patents, calculating that production would be increased by one half. It had not increased at all; opposition from the workers had made itself felt. Then Pelican, throwing himself against the new enemy, had victimized the men's leaders and expelled them from the works. There had followed two unnecessary strikes. In the end he had increased wages and sought by premiums on output to purchase willing work. The cost of production grew to an absurd extent and output decreased all the time ; the silent enmity between the workers and their employer broke out into open war. A week ago Pelican had called together the shop-stewards and offered the workers a share of the profits. At the same time, though choking with hatred, he said exceedingly gracious things—" increase output, show a little goodwill and the factory will be one-half yours." The shop-stewards refused. Very well, then, there must be a lock-out. Bliss knew that Pelican only wanted breathing space, and that he did not feel himself defeated.

" That means a strike," the manager attempted to begin once more.

" Bliss," called Pelican, as one calls a favourite dog, and started writing again.

The manager took his leave, wavering as though still expecting to be called back, but Pelican did not heed him.

Bliss leaned upon a desk and waited in silence. He smiled at his glossy boots, at his finger-nails, at the pattern of the carpet. . . . His melting Jewish eyes blinked like those of a contented cat, half-lulled to sleep by the heat and by the scratching of the pen on the paper.

"A trip to Germany," uttered Pelican without ceasing to write.

"Whereabouts?" smiled Bliss.

"Among our competitors to have a look around . . . you know what for."

Flattered, Bliss smiled. He was an industrial spy, a born intelligence man. Had there been a statesman to make use of him with his effeminate elegance, his amazing impudence, and his girlish eyes, he would have been the tool of any party or any treachery. As it was he slipped through various countries, drinking in through his half-shut smiling eyes the secrets of industrial organization, production, patents and markets, to sell them to rivals. He was curiously and devotedly grateful to Pelican, who had discovered him, a Polish refugee in wretched penury, and had set him on his feet. Now he gathered that it was a question of playing some underhand trick on their German competitors. It was the first time that Pelican had asked such a service of him.

"To Germany," repeated Bliss with his gold-stopped smile. "No further?"

"If you should have the opportunity, certainly," Pelican seemed to chew the words between his teeth. "But be back soon."

There was a moment's silence. Bliss with noiseless steps went to the window and looked out. The factory, already silent, with its great windows lit up, looked like a palace of glass. Pelican wrote on without ceasing.

" I saw your wife this morning," came from the direction of the window in a restrained and serious voice.

" Indeed," let out Pelican without moving, but the scratching of the pen ceased suddenly as if in expectation.

" She went to Stromovka Park," continued Bliss without turning round. " There she got out and took the ferry to Troja. At the castle there was waiting for her. . . ."

" Who ? " asked Pelican after a moment.

" Professor Jezek. They walked along the embankment. . . . Your wife was weeping. At the ferry they parted again."

" What were they talking about ? " said Pelican as if not asking a question.

" I don't know. He said, ' You must decide, now it is impossible, impossible like this. . . .' she wept."

" His manner——"

" His manner suggested intimacy. At the end he said, ' Till to-morrow, then.' This was at eleven o'clock this morning."

" Thanks."

The pen scratched the paper anew. Bliss

turned his half-closed eyes and smiled as before. " I will have a look at Sweden," he grinned, " the steel people there have something new."

" Pleasant journey ! " answered Pelican and handed him a cheque ; and it was evident that he still wished to work. Bliss stole quietly away. But now there is silence in the room, as though Pelican were turned to stone. Under the window the waiting chauffeur, numb with cold, can be heard stamping his feet. In the courtyard occasional voices die away as if turned to icicles—seven o'clock struck with a pleasant metallic tinkle. Pelican locked his desk, seized the telephone and called the number of his own flat.

" Is your mistress at home ? "

" Yes," replied the 'phone. " Am I to call her ? "

" No," and hanging up the receiver again he sat down.

" This morning," he repeated fixedly. " That's why Lucy was so upset . . . so . . . heaven knows. . . ."

When he had come home at midday she had been playing the piano. He had listened in the next room, and never had it occurred to him that there could be in the world anything so terrible, disturbing, ravishing, until he heard the rapture and the sobbing that she put into her playing. She had come to lunch, pale, her eyes burning feverishly. She had eaten practically nothing. They had not talked much; for generally nowadays he had nothing to say, being too much taken up with the struggle at the works of which she knew nothing. She did not hear him come or go. After lunch she played again. What dreadful force, what supreme, desperate resolution, what secret sign was she trying to find in those rolling hurricanes of sound; what intoxicant did she derive, or with whom was she conversing, in such wild ecstasy. Humbly, he bent his head. His own hard brow was callous, deafened by custom, his brain had learnt to work calmly amid the clash of steam hammers, the penetrating whine of the lathes as they rent the iron, but this outcry of tenderness and sadness which streamed from the open piano was to him like a foreign language which he strove in vain to decipher. He had waited for her to finish playing and stand up; he would have called her to him on the sofa and told her that he was tired, that what he was doing now was beyond the strength of man; he did not light a cigar lest it should annoy her. However, she had taken no notice of him; she was lost in a world of her own, and in the end he had looked at his watch and had crept out on tip-toe to come to the factory.

Pelican clenched his teeth, as though he

were biting through something with all his strength. So now Jezek, the friend of his youth. . . .

He recollected how he had introduced Jezek to his wife's drawing-room. Shaggy, bearded, round-shouldered, a somewhat ridiculous and embarrassed scholar with a child-like look of surprise behind his spectacles. He had introduced him almost by force, with good-humoured superiority, a new and amusing plaything. Jezek came rarely ; he was shy in a way, and yet soon desperately in love with his young hostess. Pelican had noticed this with the pleasure of a man of property, for he was proud of his brilliant, vivacious wife, with her imperious, impulsive ways. He had urged his friend to come oftener. Jezek had avoided him nervously, had blushed with embarrassment and torment. He would willingly never have shown himself again. Nevertheless, he returned after a time, racked, speechless, more ill at ease than ever, boundlessly happy, and torn by conflicting emotions, when his hostess picked him out from among the other guests and drew him to the piano, where, while her white hands danced a prelude, she talked, talked, talked, her half-mocking eyes fastened upon the bristling head of the unhappy professor. Even then, Pelican felt not the least compassion for the tortured man.

He had amused himself royally at the expense of his friend ; his own vitality, he felt, was so much too forceful for him ever to have imagined. . . .

The heavy clenched jaws trembled. Indeed, it was not only at the house that these things happened, Pelican remembered now for the first time. On rare occasions he accompanied his wife to concerts. Knowing that she was beside him, he was happy sitting there and thinking of his own affairs. And there too Professor Jezek was always to be seen, leaning againt the wall with head half bent. What the meaning of such music was he could not tell, but in a short time Lucy would shiver and grow pale and agitated, and then Jezek would raise his head and fix upon her a strange, wild, far-away look as though all that music were flowing from his heart. And Lucy would raise her eyes to his or drop her lids in silent response. They understood each other as it were from afar ; they conversed with one another in superhuman tones which flooded space. Then on the way home Lucy would not speak to him ; she would not even answer him, but covered her face and eyes with her furs, as if with all her strength she were trying to delay as long as possible the moment of parting with the images created by the music and—who can say what besides ?

Pelican dropped his head in his hands and groaned in anguish. Indeed, it was probably his own fault that things had gone so far! For the last few months he had really neglected Lucy; he had indeed built a wall of silence round himself, but there were so many demands made on him by work and by this terrible struggle! He had had to be at his place at the works; he must be at the bank, at a dozen board meetings. Money was needed and the business did not keep pace with the need. Money was needed . . . before all for Lucy. Lucy spent far too much. He had never told her so, but damnation! it took all his time to provide the means for her to live this life. All his time, every day. Ah, in these last few months he had felt at times that something was going on, that something had already happened. Why was Lucy sad and evasive, why pale and lost in thought, why grown so thin, and why so distant with him? He had seen all these things clearly, and with deep concern, but he had thrust them on one side by sheer force. He had had other, more urgent matters to think of. Suddenly there flashed across his mind with painful vividness the last visit of Jezek. He arrived late, with hair dishevelled, moving as if in a trance. He sat apart and spoke to no one. The young hostess, a little pale, with a tremulous smile drew near. Then Jezek rose up and as though compelling her with his eyes to advance, made her withdraw into a window recess. He said a few words to her in a whisper. Lucy inclined her head as though in a mournful " yes " and returned to the others. It was then that Pelican with uneasy apprehension had determined to be on his guard—to take precautions. But there had been so much work, so many immediate worries.

A pleasant-toned bell struck eight.

On the stone terrace by the river near Troja two people are standing ; a beautiful woman is weeping, her handkerchief pressed to her lips, and bending over her is the bearded face of a man whose teeth are bared by grief and passion. He is saying to her . . . " You must, you must resolve, no longer possible—like this——" This picture tortured Pelican with all its terrible reality. Things have gone so far with them, he said to himself, quite overwhelmed. But, good God ! what ought I to do about it ? Shall I speak to Lucy or to him ? And what am I to do if they say : " Yes, we love one another." And why ask that, when it is so clear already ? His heavy hands contracted on the cover of the desk—he thought that he was going to be seized by a mad fit of rage and fury, but instead a boundless weariness seemed to smother him. From this desk of his he had decided many contests. From here he had commanded men and events; here he had parried and given so many blows with the startling instantaneous promptitude of a well-trained boxer. And now with horror and with a kind of gloomy hatred of himself he felt that he was not capable of answering this blow in any way. In his weakness he measured the completeness of his defeat. " Something must happen, I will do something," he repeated stubbornly. But suddenly he seemed again to see Lucy at the piano with her eyes feverish and clouded; Lucy pale and shrinking, the beautiful woman on the terrace by the river, and once again he was borne down by a flood of painful and intolerable helplessness.

At last he overcame this weakness and managed to stand up and go down to his car. The automobile glided silently to the centre of Prague. Then Pelican's eyes grew suddenly bloodshot and he began to shout to the driver, " Faster, faster ! "

He foamed and snorted in a sudden flood of fury. He felt that he must fly like a projectile through the people, crush them, rush on, colliding against some obstacle with a frightful crash. " Faster ! faster ! You idiot of a driver, who do you avoid them ? " The astonished chauffeur put his car to top speed, the horn sounded without ceasing, there were cries from the poeple; they had almost run over a man.

He entered his home in apparent calm. Supper passed in strained silence. Lucy, depressed and absorbed in her own thoughts, did not speak. She had eaten only a few mouthfuls when she wished to go. " Wait," said Pelican and with his cigar alight came over to her and looked into her eyes.

Lucy raised to meet his her eyes which were filled with sudden opposition and fear. " Let me go," she begged and pretended to cough as though the smoke choked her.

" You are coughing, Lucy," he said, not taking his eyes from her, " you must go away from here."

" Where to ? " she whispered in terror.

" To Italy, to the sea, anywhere. You must go to the baths. When can you start ? "

" I won't go away," she said vehemently. " I don't need to go away anywhere ! Really there is nothing the matter with me ! "

" You are pale," he went on with a steady inquiring gaze. " It does not suit you here. You must have two or three years' cure."

" No, no, no, I won't go away anywhere," she cried in dreadful anguish. " No ! please, please ! I will not go," she exclaimed in a voice full of tears, and ran from the room in order not to burst out weeping.

Pelican with his shoulders hunched went to his study.

That night, in the ante-room of the master's bedroom an old servant was waiting to prepare the evening bath for him. It was midnight and his master had not come. The servant stole to the door of the study on tip-toe, and listened. He heard heavy regular steps from wall to wall, up and down unendingly. Then he went back to his lackey's arm-chair and fell into a broken sleep, waking every now and then with the cold. At about half-past three he started from a deep sleep to see his master getting into a fur coat. He ran to him stammering apologies for having fallen asleep.

"I must go away," interrupted Pelican. "I shall be back this evening."

"Shall I call the car, sir?" asked the servant.

"No need." Pelican went on foot to the nearest railway station. It was freezing slightly; the street was empty as in a dream, and desolate with the loneliness of death. At the station some people were lying asleep on the seats and others, freezing patiently in silence, sat huddled together like dumb animals. Pelican picked out on the " departure " board the first train to anywhere and went striding up and down the long platform. Thus occupied, he forgot all about his train, selected another and was off at last in an empty carriage, he knew not where. It was a still night; he turned off the light and settled himself in a corner.

Everything combined to overwhelm him in floods of infinite weariness. Each rattle of the train seemed to bring another and yet another wave of weakness; he was sunk in deadly depression and at the same time in extreme ease, as though for the first time for years he were resting profoundly and passively. He did not defend himself. For the first time in his life he accepted a blow, feeling with amazement something like satisfaction that the deadly wound went so deep. He had come right away from home to be alone for a whole day, so that he might consider clearly, and without being disturbed, what was to be done about Lucy, how to deal with this dreadful entanglement, but now he was incapable of decision and hardly desired anything more than to remain passively entranced by his own weakness. Low down in the sky glimmered the first glow of the new day. People were waking up, abandoning with regret their warm unconsciousness. Now—now Lucy is still asleep. He sees her wide pillow, her fair hair pressed beneath her cheek, perhaps still wet with tears, the tears of a tired child. She is pale and beautiful, ah, Lucy! truly such weakness is nothing else but love! In heaven's name, what decision did I want to arrive at? Indeed, there can be no doubt that I love you still!

Do something! do something! do something! pounded the clanging wheels emphatically. No! No! No! What is to be done? Why, there is nothing to be done but to love again! But if Lucy be unhappy, something must be done to prevent it. Do something! do something! do something! Wait a little, Lucy, only wait a little, I will show you what love is. You must be happy and even if I . . . Is there any decision to make at all? If I love her, then I must prove it. What sacrifice is great enough to offer her?

Over the country the dawn began.

Quietly, powerfully, beat the heart of the man bearing its great sorrow. Lucy, Lucy, I will give you back your freedom; follow your love and be happy. I will make even this sacrifice. You are frail and beautiful—go, Lucy, and be happier. Landscape followed landscape; the powerful, stubborn forehead was pressed against the frozen pane that he might overcome the intoxicating pain, and his heart seemed, already, through a wide, gaping wound, to drink in the peace of a decision made.

"I will tell her this evening," meditated Pelican, "I will tell her that we will separate. After her first alarm she will agree to it. Inside six months she will be happy. Jezek will satisfy her every desire; he will understand her better than I, and Lucy will be. . . ."

Pelican jumped as though he had been struck. How on earth could Lucy be happy in poverty? Lucy, who is luxury itself; Lucy, the very essence of expensive whims; Lucy, who had been introduced to his own wealthy home from all the luxury of a great mercantile family just before her father's bankruptcy. Lucy, who from some kind of instinct, passion or need of her being, from simplicity or from some other cause, must throw about ridiculously large sums of money. In fact, all that Jezek could earn for her would not be enough for one frock! . . . But what does it matter, he objected to himself. In the case of a separation, I will pay alimony, and I will give her as much——

But as to alimony, he recollected suddenly, of course she will be marrying Jezek and naturally I cannot pay. She cannot possibly marry Jezek! She must remain free, so that she can go on receiving at my hands. But what will become of her? The intimacy with Jezek will naturally take its course. If they do not marry, it will lead to publicity . . . an open liaison. The society in which she lives will make her feel her position; they will cast her out and humiliate her. And she herself, haughty, spirited Lucy, will suffer terribly in her own mind. She has been brought up simply with strict ideas. . . . That cannot be! Let us separate and let her marry Jezek and learn to live in poverty if she can; and from time to time, thought Pelican, I will offer Jezek an allowance. Then he felt ashamed; that was something which Jezek really could not accept!

Full of perplexity he jumped out of the train at the first station. He did not know in the least where he was. He could not remain sitting any longer. To bring himself back to his senses he must flee over the black fields striped with hard snow. The dawn was grey and damp. No sooner was Pelican out of the station, than he seated himself on a stone by the highroad and recommenced his meditating.

I might perhaps say to her: I will go away from you, but I give you so much as a dowry, you understand? She could then live on the interest. Then she would be able to marry! Quickly he reckoned how much money he could realize. There was no help that way. He lived, as a matter of fact, from day to day. No use, Lucy, you must economize. You will have to make your own clothes, you will stand over the kitchen range. Each evening you will count up with anxiety how much you have spent.

He began to shiver with the cold. He stood

up and proceeded at random along the road. Lucy, Lucy, what am I to do about you? Really I could not leave you to such penury! No, that is not for you. Ah, child, you do not know how matter-of-fact and how exacting is poverty! Be sensible, Lucy; just think of all you are accustomed to have—— Deep in painful meditation, he grew warm with quick walking. He did not know himself how it came about, but he began to form new plans on a grand scale, some prodigious industrial campaign which would throw fresh millions into his hands. In a flash he saw the necessary operations and details, he calculated, he broke down future opposition. Through it all there stirred the wild idea that perhaps Lucy would look at everything in a different light if he were to overwhelm her with new and yet greater riches. He stopped short, breathless, at the top of a hill which he had taken in one rush. Neither the highroad nor the railroad was to be seen now. All around undulated the russet-coloured hills of southern Bohemia, alternating with black woods. He set out across the fields, frozen and weary beyond measure. At last he reached a village and tumbled into the nearest inn.

He was alone in the low-ceilinged tap-room, served by a scrubby boy who brought him reddish tea with rum, which smelt of snuff.

He drank down the scalding abomination at one gulp and thawed by degrees back to life. No! Lucy shall not suffer. It is to prevent that, Lucy, that I am here. Perhaps at this very moment she is waking up ; she is getting up already, looking like a little child, and she remembers yesterday's sorrow. He was so weary that he felt himself as old as though he were her father. You shall not go to live in poverty, Lucy ; nothing, nothing must happen. Neither by word nor behaviour will I let it be seen that I know anything. Live in your luxurious dream, love, do what you wish. After all, I am away from home the whole day, and can give you nothing but riches. Have everything, Lucy, everything that you wish, and be happy. Your proud heart will keep you from sinning too seriously. . . .

At intervals the boy came in from the passage with unkind caution. What did he want here, this big gentleman in the fur coat, sitting there in the corner, twisting his empty glass in his fingers, and smiling away to himself? Why didn't he pay and take himself off?

But that is impossible, Pelican suddenly realized with a shock. Lucy already suffers from her intimacy with Jezek, already now, when there is scarcely anything between them but vain talk. Already she runs away from me in guilty fear and weeps from exaggerated sensitiveness. What will she come to to-morrow or the day after when things have gone farther ? Why, Lucy, ardent and haughty Lucy, could she bear—even—even—faithlessness ? She would be overwhelmed by self-abasement, torn by terror and disgrace to the depths of her heart ! Can I allow that ? Pelican asked himself in anguish. Why—can I not prevent it in any way——?

" Don't you wish to pay ? " asked the youth gloomily.

Pelican pulled out his watch. It was eleven o'clock. " At what time does the first train go to Prague ? "

" At half-past eleven."

" How far is it to the station ? "

" An hour's walk."

" Can I get a car ? "

" No."

Eleven o'clock, remembered Pelican. Now, exactly at this moment they are to meet on the Embankment by Troja Castle. He saw a long stone terrace. Lucy turning away to the grey water and weeping into her handkerchief. Perhaps even now they are making up their minds, madly, unreasoningly, perhaps foolish Lucy is choosing her fate now, while I here. . . .

He sprang to his feet, bereft of reason. " You must get me a car." The youth went out grumbling.

Pelican took his stand in front of the inn, his heart beating, his watch in his hand. Good God! is no one ever coming? He raged impatiently; ten minutes passed without result. At last there rattled up a rustic little cart, drawn by a white pony. Pelican threw himself into it, crying: " Quickly! I will give you anything you like to ask if you catch the train! "

" Surely," replied the grey-haired driver as he mildly urged on his steed.

Up hill and down, along the highroad jogged the pony. " Faster! " Pelican would say, and each time the old man would gently pull the reins and the little white mare would swing her legs a little more quickly. At last a powerful form arose behind the old man, snatched the reins and whip from him, and flogged, flogged, flogged the mare, over the head, round the legs and along the back. The wretched animal sprang forward and dashed along the road, stung to the quick. There is the railway at last, but at a bend in the road one of the back-wheels collided with a milestone, the stone was uprooted, the cart turned on its side. The wheel broke off like a toy and the little cart, dropping on to its belly, abandoned the race. Pelican shouted with rage, struck the mare on the jaw with his fist and just as he was, in his fur coat, ran at top speed to the station. The train was drawing up to the platform.

"Do something, do something, do something," thudded the throbbing wheels. In the crowded carriage, Pelican, covered with perspiration, stamped and clenched his fists in mad fits of impatience. How slowly it goes, slowly, slowly, compared with the human will. Stations glided away ; behind them sped tree-lined avenues, a little bridge, woods—one thing after another—telegraph poles. . . . Pelican pulled down the window and looked straight down at the wheels of the train. Here at least the endless belt of gravel and sleepers rushed along drunkenly, furiously, in blind speed as in a feverish dream.

Prague ! Pelican ran from the station and drove straight to Jezek's address. Breathlessly he rang at the door.

"The professor's not at home," the landlady declared, "but he will be in to luncheon, probably about half-past two."

"I'll wait," muttered Pelican, and sat down in Jezek's room.

Three o'clock had struck long since and it was drawing near four. Jezek had not returned. In the room it began to grow dark. Pelican breathed hoarsely as though someone were pursuing him. Perhaps already he was too late. At last, long past four, the door flew open and Jezek stood on the threshold. He recognized Pelican and grew rigid.

"You—waiting here," he gasped in something that could hardly be called a voice. . . . "Why !—you went away ! "

Pelican suddenly recovered his balance. "How do you know that I went away ? " he asked coolly.

Jezek understood that he had said too much. He flushed crimson and his brow grew moist with anxiety, but he said nothing.

"I have come back now," began Pelican after a while, "and there is a matter which I wish to straighten out. Do you mind if I smoke ? "

Jezek was silent. His heart beat so loudly that he felt that it must be audible, and his trembling fingers drummed a surreptitious tattoo on the table. The tiny flame of the match lit up clearly the savage face of Pelican with its half-shut eyes and brutal jaws.

"To cut matters short," said Pelican, " there must be an end to this, you understand ? You will ask for a transfer from Prague."

Jezek still stood silent.

" My wife must be left in peace," said Pelican. " I trust you will not dare to write to her— from the scene of your future labours."

" I will not go away from here," broke out Jezek, in a quivering voice. " Do what you please, I will not go away. Oh, I know you think differently. . . . You don't understand the situation ! You don't understand at all. . . ."

" I understand nothing," said Pelican, " except this, that there must be an end. All this leads to nothing. You must go away."

Jezek sprang to his feet. " Give her back her freedom," he rasped passionately, " release her, release her from your golden cage ! It is not for myself that I am asking ; but have mercy on her ! Man, for once in your life have a heart ! Don't you feel that she cannot endure you, that she is desperate in your presence ? What is your object in keeping her bound ? You two have not an idea in common, not one single interest ! Tell me, have you anything to say to her, anything more to give her than . . . money ? "

" No," came the reply from out of the darkness.

" Give her back her freedom ! I know— she knows, that you are fond—that you may be fond—of her in your own way, but that is not it . . . and then these last few months . . . you two have been strangers to each other ! If only you would consent to a separation ! "

" Let her ask for that herself."

" Ah, why will you not understand ? She has not the courage, she cannot say it to you herself. . . . You are so generous to her !

You do not understand her, you do not know how sensitive she is ; she would sooner die than tell you. She is such a tender, delicate thing—so dependent on others ! She could not do such a thing herself. . . . But suppose you were to say to her yourself that you were setting her free ! It is a question of her happiness. . . . Pelican, I know that you are not accustomed to all this talk about love. For you it is all probably nothing more than a lot of phrases . . . and so . . . really . . . you cannot understand such a woman ! You yourself are not really happy either ! Tell me, what does she give you of herself ? What can she be to you ? You merely torture her with your attentions—how can it be that you don't feel how terrible that is ? "

" You would marry her, then ? " muttered Pelican.

" I am not—oh God !—how gladly," gasped Jezek, intensely relieved and full of hope. " If only she consents ! I would think of nothing but her happiness. . . . If only you knew how we understand each other. If she would but decide," he was almost weeping with joy as he spoke, " I would do anything for her ! . . . Really, I have almost lost my senses ; I breathe for her—Man, you don't know . . . I never thought that it was possible to love so much ! "

" How much do you get ? "

" What did you say ? " questioned Jezek, confused.

" What income have you ? "

" As for that," stammered Jezek at a loss, " you know I have not much—but she would economize ; we have talked that over already. . . . If only you could know of how little importance money is to us ! That is something you don't understand, Pelican, there are other and greater things. . . . With her, money does not count. You see, she doesn't even want to talk of how it will be . . . afterwards. Really she absolutely despises money ! "

" But you ! What do *you* think ? "

" I ? Oh, you see, you are of a different type from us ; you are only able to think of your material affairs. . . . Lucy is so much above you. She would not take even a pin of yours away with her, if you let her go. Above all, I want her to bring nothing, you understand ? It would be an entirely new life for her."

The red tip of the cigar rose up. " What a pity," said Pelican. " I would have listened to you longer with pleasure, but I must go to the works. So listen to me now a moment, Jezek."

" Really your wealth enslaves her."

" Yes. Now, you will ask for that transfer— good-bye—Jezek. And if you come to our house, don't be surprised if you are watched.

And don't walk on the embankment if you don't want to be thrown into the river. You will not speak to my wife any more."

Jezek was breathing with difficulty. "I will not go from Prague."

"Then she shall go. If you want to force matters to that point. . . . But you will not meet my wife again—Good-bye!"

A few minutes later, when the porter's wife was coming down from the top of the house, she found a gentleman in a fur coat seated on the stairs.

"Are you ill?" she asked sympathetically.

"Yes—no——" said the gentleman, as if he was only just waking up. "Please call me a cab."

She ran for a cab, and as he was climbing into it heavily it occurred to her that he was probably drunk. Pelican gave the driver the address of his home, but after a few moments he tapped the man on the shoulder: "Turn back, I am going to the works."

TWO FATHERS

SINCE morning the square had been blazing like a burning hot oven under the cloudless sky. White gables with arcades beneath cactus and geranium blooming in the windows ; and a reddish coloured little dog scratching himself on the pavement. The frowning façades of well-to-do houses breathed coolness into the glaring day ; a comfortable gloom peered from within through the great dark panes of the closed windows. In front of the apothecary's house the St. Bernard dog lay sleeping like a sphinx. It was quiet, always quiet in this square ; quiet when it rained, quiet in the midday heat, quiet on Sundays, quiet on week-days. The church, like some huge, sheer ship, rose up in the middle of the square. It was there that the little girl used to walk while she lived.

She died, and never had the little town seen such grief as the grief of her father. For the last few days before she died he never left her bedside : only while she slept he would stand at the window and look out on the square. It was there that he used to walk with her while she lived, going hand in hand with her and chatting ; the apothecary's St. Bernard always swept the ground with his heavy tail and stood up for her to stroke him. The old apothecary would reach across to a glass jar and give her a handful of grey throat lozenges. The little girl used to spit them out afterwards with disgust, and her poor little fingers would be smeared and sticky for a long time.

He used to walk with her down there and on to the river. She was afraid of some houses and would never say why ; she was afraid of people and of mischievous dogs, of wells with buckets, of bridges, beggars, and horses ; she was afraid of the river and of engines. At every shudder of fear she squeezed her father's hand and he responded with a strong, protective clasp : " Don't be frightened, I'm here." He would go with her here on woodland walks and roll cones down the slope with affected gaiety ; the child never asked questions about anything. Everyone knew them : he the grave father, stout, bent, and so taken up with her ; she the badly-dressed six-year-old girl with light hair and a pinched face. The children used to call after her " skinny-ninny " ; then he would flush, be pained and go and complain to their parents. That is how their walks used to be.

The St. Bernard got up and looked round. She was ill for three weeks and then died. A few beggar-women stood in front of the house of mourning; the funeral guests assembled, stood baking for a time in the square, and then went in. The musicians were waiting already, and the choirboys with crosses and lanterns; four workmen from the father's workshop, in new black suits, brought the bier covered with a long pall, little girls in white came, half-nervous and half-pleased, the choir arrived with music-sheets under their arms, tall, laughing young women with light-coloured dresses and bunches of flowers; gradually the leading folk of the town assembled, wearing long black coats and silken skirts, heavy top-hats, grave and solemn faces; the whole town came, since the father was a man of means and importance there. At last came the dean with two priests in white canonicals signifying heavenly joys. Upstairs in the large drawing-room lay the little girl, with a wreath on her fair hair and a broken candle in her little waxen hands.

It was quiet in the square and the St. Bernard was lying down with his head raised towards the hushed house. Then through the window came the powerful voice of the priest: "*Sit nomen Domini.*" The beggar-women fell on their knees. "*Laudate pueri Dominum : laudate nomen Domini.*" The male choir joined in, "*Sit nomen Domini benedictum.*" The beggar-women in front of the house set up a mumbled confused praying which slowly shaped itself into the words of the *Pater noster.* "*Hic accipiet,*" rang the powerful voice of the dean. "*Kyrie eleison,*" "*Christe eleison,*" "*Kyrie eleison. Et ne nos inducas in tentationem.*" "*Sed libera nos a malo.*" The St. Bernard, with drooping tail, slunk home. It was silent in the house, so that even the beggars were quiet. Only the fountain murmured in the centre of the square.

The little girl was dead; she had been a sickly child and not even pretty, she was afraid of the broad square, she was afraid of the big dog and the fountain which for her had no bottom; she went through life hanging on to her father's hand, lay ill in his arms, and now, praised be the Lord, for she has died in her poor little sixth year to go and be an angel.

Across the sweltering square the black procession made its way: choristers with crosses and lanterns, wailing music, little girls with wreaths of rosemary, each carrying a broken candle on a cushion, priests with lighted candles, and then the little coffin itself, so light amid all that sumptuous display, stiff, broad ribbons, waxen wreaths and bands of black crape, the father with bent head and face almost obliterated with grief, the pale, under-sized mother under her black veil, and then the people, black and gloomy, with bald heads in the glare of the sun, with white handker-chiefs, a slow-moving, whispering crowd, and in the rear, like a separate and muttering island, the beggars with their never-ending prayer.

Along the parched, hollow path the procession climbed to the Calvary of human sorrows. Behind the bare wall lay the new cemetery, white and dry, the sandy ground of the dead, where nothing grew but white crosses, lilies made of metal and the lean tower of the cemetery chapel. All bare and bleached like bones. A white, dead noon. A white, burning path. The little coffin mounted up and drew after it the mournful procession ; a little coffin, a little dead body in its white shroud with the broken candle ; there where she used to walk hand in hand with her father—

—Poor fellow, he had loved her so dearly ! He had married late and looked forward to the coming of the first child ; and then, you know of course, there came the new choir-leader, and the wife lost her head about him. All the town knew about it. That was how this fair-haired girlie came to be born to dark-haired parents ; she was exactly like that organist fellow, the very image of him.   She absolutely pointed to her own real father.

The light little coffin seemed changed into lead ; the bearers halted and placed the bier on the ground. Yes, just as far as here she used to walk with her father ; here they used to sit and look down on to the road with the caravans of travelling players, farm waggons, and dog-carts, looking down on the streets and guessing who was going by——

The whole town knew whom the mother was carrying on with, only the husband was blind ; he had his child, the light-haired and pale-eyed little girl whom he fussed over while his wife ran round having jealous quarrels with every young woman whom her musician taught to pound on the keys. Finally he had to break with her if he wasn't to lose all his lessons on her account ; and then he let anyone who asked for it have her letters to read, and everyone asked.

The music again wailed out a doleful march, and the slow procession wound heavily upwards to the sound of bells. The little lady in the veil, with lips sharply pressed together, stumbled over the hem of her skirt ; she was holding herself erect to face all those glances, before she shut herself up at home again, with her endless embroidery, by the window, pale with loneliness and hatred.

Yes, he had abandoned her after that, and so she stayed there with this child coldly repulsive to her, and her husband who now had no thought but for that impassive little girl who was not his. He was attached to her with the full force of his slow-witted affection; and the little town really did not know whether to laugh at or pity him when he brought her, queerly dressed, pale and wide-eyed, out from the chilly rooms of the house into the square. Then the bells ceased with a short peal.

The little coffin was knocking at the gate of eternity. It was resting on planks over the open grave in the middle of the great, speechless crowd; in the dead silence only the choir rustled music-books and the dean slowly turned over the leaves of a little book bound in black. In the crowd a child burst out crying. The thin shadow of the tower cut across the burning ground belonging to the dead. Just a year ago they had begun to bury here; and perhaps the cemetery was too large, perhaps they would never fill it, perhaps the grass would never grow there, perhaps it must remain for all eternity as empty and bare. The procession breathed heavily in anxiety. What was happening? Why didn't they begin? The silence drew out painfully, heavily, oppressively—

" *Laudate Dominum de coelis, laudate eum in excelsis !* " " *Laudate eum omnes angeli eius,* " chanted the choir, "*Laudate eum omnes virtutes eius*." The crowd breathed again. "*Laudate eum sol et luna ; laudate eum stellae et lumen*." "*Laudate eum coeli coelorum*." A faint breeze, as though waked by the chorus of male voices, wafted relief to the pale faces ; a cloud of incense rose, ribbons and wreaths rustled, and from the grave breathed the chill of clay. The father stared motionless at the coffin, bending over as if he would fall ; people stood on tip-toe to see him better ; now, now the moment of parting had come.

"*Kyrie eleison*." "*Christe eleison*." "*Kyrie eleison*." The young priest swung the censer, its fine chains rattled softly, the smoke rose and quivered—"*Oremus*." The wide, burning sky stretched dully over the white cemetery, for one second of painful eternity there was only the beating of hearts in the tension of a terrible, great and agonizing moment. "*Per omnia saecula saeculorum. Amen*." Drops of holy water were sprinkled on the little coffin ; the father fell on his knees sobbing aloud ; the coffin slowly descended into the grave and the choir broke sweetly, mournfully and softly into the chorale " God has called."

The little lady in the veil listened as if transfixed. She knew only too well that rich, smooth, self-satisfied, self-complacent voice. Once she had heard it under other circumstances and had melted passionately under its almost material contact. The whole of the little town listened with bowed heads : the choir-leader was singing alone with Marie, the chief of the women singers, the Venus of the place, a tall, handsome girl. Only these two voices were heard out of all the choir. It was said that this Marie was running after him. The two voices blended and mingled lovingly. in the broad sunlight; the dean himself listened with closed eyes ; the little lady broke into convulsive weeping ; the little blue cloud of incense rose to the sky, and softly, very softly the finale floated over the cemetery. The dean awoke as if from a dream and bent down to the earth.

One, two, three ; everyone pressed forward to the open grave where the father was kneeling on the piled-up clay and sobbing as though he could never stop. They each threw their three clods into the grave and would have liked to be gone. They only waited until the father should rise so as to press his hand. The priests fidgeted a little, they had still to go to the chapel again ; the grave-digger blew his nose noisily and began to shovel the dry and burning clay into the grave. The whole assembly stood in perplexed, helpless silence.

Then the choir broke into a ripple of laughter.

The choir-leader's eyes twinkled, glad that his joke had told. Pale Agnes blushed, Matilda bit her handkerchief, and Marie doubled up and exploded soundlessly. The choir-master smoothed his moustache and hair with a satisfied air, bent over to Marie and whispered something to her. Marie giggled and stepped back. The whole company looked round, half-amused and half-indignant.

Suddenly the father rose, trembling, and tried to speak. " To you, you all—who have shown to my beloved little daughter—my only child——" But he could get no further; he sobbed, and without offering his hand to any-one, moved away as if in a dream. There was a general stir. Then as the priests passed into the chapel the assembly broke up and dispersed. Some of them hastily marked the graves of their departed with three crosses, others paused for a time before some monument, and scarcely anyone waited for the end of the ceremony; only the choir-leader with Marie and the choir-girls passed with a loud laugh into the chancel of the cemetery chapel.

A few women in black were praying by the graves, they wiped their eyes and arranged the poor withered flowers.

From the open doors of the chapel floated the voice of the dean : " *Benedicite omnia opera Domini Domino.*"

" *Benedicite angeli Domini Domino*," chimed in the choir-leader.

" *Benedicite coeli Domino.*"

The grave-digger, with heaped-up spadefuls, was burying the child of two fathers.

"D, Mary, D," repeated Olga with mechanical patience.

Little Mary reluctantly hammered out a very easy study on the piano : they had been at that piece already a fortnight and the longer time they spent the worse was the result. That detested childish tune haunted Olga even in her dreams.

"D, Mary, be careful : C D G D," Olga hummed it with a feeble voice and played it over. "Take more pains : C D G D,—but, Mary, D—D, why do you persist in playing E ? "

Mary did not know why she was playing badly, she only knew that she was compelled to play : her eyes flashed with hatred, she kicked against the stool and at the earliest possible moment she would run to papa ; meanwhile she purposely played E again and again. Olga gave up attending and gazed out of the window with eyes of anguish. The sun was shining, the great trees in the park waved in a hot breeze, but there was no liberty in the park nor even in the rough fields beyond—ah, when would the lesson be up? And E again and again!

"D, Mary, D," repeated Olga most despairingly, and suddenly burst out, "you will never know how to play."

The little girl drew herself up, scorched Olga with a glance of ancestral pride, and retorted—"Why don't you say that before papa?"

Olga bit her lips. "Play," she cried with undue sharpness, noticing the child's glance of hatred, and started to count with impatient emphasis, "one, two, three, four; one, two, three, four; one, two, three, four; C D G D. Badly. One, two, three, four——"

The door of the drawing-room was shaking. No doubt the old count was behind it again so as to listen. Olga subdued her voice.

"One, two, three, four. C D G D. Very well, Mary." It was certainly not well, but the old count was listening. "One, two, three, four. Now it is quite well. It is really not so difficult, eh? One, two——"

The door flew open and the lame count entered, clattering along with his stick.

"*Ha ha, Mary, wie geht's? Hast du schön gespielt? Eh, miss?*"

"Oh yes, my lord," asserted Olga heartily, rising from the piano.

"*Mary, du hast Talent,*" cried the crippled old

man, and all at once—it was almost terrible to look at—he fell heavily on his knees with a hollow sound on the floor, and with a kind of sobbing whine kissed his child on the neck with noisy, wild caresses. "*Du hast Talent,*" he murmured, "*du bist so gescheit, Mary, so gescheit ! Sag'mal, was soll dir dein Papa schenken ?*"

"*Danke, nichts,*" replied Mary, wriggling her sensitive little shoulders beneath his caresses, "*ich möchte nur——*"

"*Was, was möchtest du ?*" babbled the count enthusiastically.

"*Ich möchte nur nit so viel Stunden haben,*" ejaculated Mary.

"*Ha ha, natürlich,*" laughed the count, enchanted, "*nein, wie gescheit bist du !* Isn't she, miss ?"

"Yes," breathed Olga.

"*Wie gescheit!*" repeated the old man and wanted to stand up. Olga sprang to help him. "Let me be," cried the count fiercely, and standing on knee and hand like an animal tried to rise. Olga turned away. Then five convulsive fingers gripped her arm, and leaning his whole weight thereon the old count stood up. Olga for a wonder did not stumble under the weight of this huge, apoplectic, fearful body ; it was above her courage. Little Mary laughed.

The count straightened himself, put on his glasses, and gazed at Olga with surprise as though he had not seen her before.

" Miss Olga."

" Please ? " breathed the girl.

Then in English. " Miss Olga, you speak too much during the lesson : you confound the child by your eternal admonishing. You will make me this pleasure to be a little kinder."

" Yes, sir," whispered Olga, blushing to her hair. Mary understood that papa was scolding Olga, and loftily feigned that it did not concern her.

" Very well, good morning, miss," concluded the count.

Olga bowed and was going out, when, on the way, turning with flashing eyes, she remarked, " Mary, you might salute when I go out."

" *Ja, mein Kind, das kannst du,*" assented the old count benevolently. Mary grinned and flung off a curtsey with lightning speed.

Scarcely was Olga beyond the door when she pressed her hand to her forehead. " Oh heavens, I cannor bear it, I cannot ! For five months not a day or even an hour has passed that they have not tormented me. . . . But really they don't torment me," she said to herself as she proceeded along the chilly hall with her palms to her temples. " I am a stranger and a hired person and no one thinks of me. It's only the way they are made, God, and nowhere is one so solitary as among strange people. But Mary is wicked," cried something fiercely within her, " and hates me ; she wants to annoy me and is proud and affronts me, but Mary is wicked. The child that I wanted to love. The child with whom I spend the whole day long, the whole day. Heavens, how many years of this ? "

Two chambermaids were giggling in the passage. As soon as they noticed Olga they were silent and saluted her with oblique glances. Through sheer jealousy Olga very nearly rounded on them for their laughing ; she would have liked to order them about in a lofty way, but did not know how. If at least she were in the servants' hall with these girls, it occurred to her ; squeaking well into the night, gossiping and chasing each other, and Franz, the lackey with them every moment one or other of them squealing—oh dear, how disgusting it was ! A most unpleasant memory forced itself on her ; yesterday she surprised Franz with the scullery-maid in an empty guest-room by her bedroom ; she could have struck him with her little passionate fist on his face with its idiotic grin as he drew back from the girl. She buried her fingers in her face. No, no, I can't endure it. C D G D, C D G D—

But these servant girls at least amuse themselves. At least they are not so lonely, they do not take their meals with gentlefolk, they babble the whole day and in the evening sing softly out in the yard. If at least they received me among themselves in the evening. Sweetly, melodiously floated across her mind what they were singing as a part-song yesterday under the old linden—

> only my heart aches,
> I could weep at once.

She listened at her window with eyes full of tears and sang with them in a demi-voice; all was forgiven to them and the hand of ardent friendship was extended to them. Girls, indeed, I am the same as you. Even I am a serving maid and the most unhappy of all of you.

"The most unhappy," repeated Olga to herself as she passed along the hall. "How did the count put it?" 'Miss Olga, you speak too much during the lessons: you confound the child by your eternal admonishing. You will do me the pleasure to be a little kinder.'" She repeated this word for word, so as not to lose a drop of bitterness. She clenched her fist, burning with wrath and pain. Yes, that was her weakness: she took her task of governess too seriously. She came to the castle with glowing enthusiasm, already in love with the little girl to be entrusted to her. She passionately threw herself into the instruction, zealous, pedantic, and full of knowledge; she boundlessly believed in the importance of education, but now she was only drudging with tiresome Mary bits of arithmetic and grammar, always being put out, hammering her knuckles on the table and then leaving the schoolroom in tears, while Mary remained triumphantly with her defiance and mistakes. At first she used to play with Mary with exuberance and unrestrained heartiness, childishly taken up with her toys; at length she found that she was making a sport of herself before the cold, mockingly bored glance of the child, and so much for games—and Olga followed at the heels of her little charge like a shadow, not knowing what to say to her or how to amuse her. Accepting the task as a sacred trust she had come here, filled with a sentiment of love, gentleness and patience; now look at her flaming eyes, listen how violently and unevenly her heart beat; that heart which only can feel pain and no love at all. " Be—a little—kinder," repeated Olga to herself trembling: Oh, heaven, can I do that any longer ?

With cheeks flaming with excitement she ran along through rows of figures in tin, knights in armour, at which she used to laugh.

A thousand things occurred to her to say to the count in reply to his reprimand; expressions full of dignity rushed to her mind, replies decisive and proud, which would make her for ever a person of weight in that house. My lord count, she might say with head erect, I know what I want: I want Mary to learn strict understanding of everything and to teach her self-control; I want to make of her someone who will not allow herself to commit faults. Lord count, it is not a matter of false piano notes but of false training; I cannot love Mary and take no heed of her faults; but if I love her I will be as severe as I am to myself. She became almost cheerful when she said it all with glistening eyes, with her heart inflamed by a recent pain; then she felt relieved, and firmly resolved that soon, to-morrow, she would have it out with the count. The count himself was not so bad after all, he had his generous moments, and after all he suffered so much. If only he had not those terrible light, domineering eyes staring behind his eyeglasses.

She passed before the castle, dazzled by the sunlight: the pavement glistened, as it had been sprinkled some time before, and a damp odour rose.

"Look out, miss," cried the shrill voice of Oswald, and at the same instant a wet football bounded against Olga's white dress. Oswald started chuckling, but stopped when he saw the poor girl looked shocked. The skirt was entirely splashed with mud; Olga raised it and without a word of reproach began to sob. Oswald blushed and stammered: "I did not see you, miss."

"Beg your pardon, miss," cried in English Oswald's tutor, Mr. Kennedy, who in white shirt and trousers was lolling on the grass plot; with a single movement he bounded up, gave Oswald a cuff on the head and then threw himself down again. Olga merely regarded her skirt: she was so fond of this white dress. Without a word she turned and went home, controlling herself with all her might so that tears should not burst out as she walked.

Her throat already quivered with the desire to weep, when she opened the door of her room. There she stood in horror, hardly understanding what was going forward; the countess was seated in the arm-chair in the middle of the room, and the chamber-maid in front of her was rummaging through Olga's own wardrobe.

"*Ah, c'est vous,*" greeted the countess without looking round.

"*Oui, madame la comtesse,*" Olga forced out of herself, scarcely breathing, with staring eyes.

The chambermaid pulled out a whole armful of clothes.

" My lady, it's not here really."

" Very well then," replied the countess, heavily rising to go out. The amazed Olga did not think to give way as she approached the door. The countess halted three paces before her. " *Mademoiselle ?* "

" *Oui, madame.* "

" *Vous n'attendez pas, peut-être, que je m'ex-cuse ?* "

" *Non, non, madame,* " cried the girl.

" *Alors il n'y a pas pourquoi me barrer le passage,* " grumbled the countess with her guttural *r*.

" *Ah pardon, madame la comtesse,* " murmured Olga swiftly making way. The countess and chambermaid went out : there remained only articles of clothing scattered on the table and bed.

Olga sat on the chair like a wooden image : tears were denied her. They had been looking through her wardrobe as though she were some thieving servant.

" Perhaps you are not waiting for me to apologise ? "

No, no, countess : heaven defend you from begging pardon of a girl who is in your pay. Here are my pockets, there is my purse : look through everything, so as to see what I have stolen. I am poor and certainly dishonest. Olga gazed fixedly on the floor. Now at last she was aware why so often she had found her dresses and linen sort of thrown about. And I eat with them at the same table, give answer, smile, make one of the company, force myself to be cheerful. Olga was overwhelmed with boundless humiliation. Her eyes were widely staring and tearless, her clenched hands pressed against her breast; there was no capacity for thought, only her heart beat painfully and dreadfully.

A fly settled on her clasped hand, rubbed its tiny head, cleaned its wings and ran to and fro, but the hands did not move. Now and then a hoof stamped or a chain rattled in the stable. Crockery rang in the pantry, a hawk shrieked over the park, and a train whistled at a distant bend. At length it seemed too long even for the fly, which twitched its wings and flew through the open window. Absolute silence fell upon the castle.

One, two, three, four. Four o'clock. Noisily yawning, a cookmaid came to prepare tea. Rapid steps were heard in the yard, the windlass creaked at the well, and a certain haste was noticeable in the house. Olga rose, passed her hands over her brow as if memory failed her, and set herself to arrange neatly the dresses on the table. Then she knelt at the linen-press, took out linen and laid it on the bed. She put her little books on the chairs, and when quite ready stood above them all as over the ruins of Jerusalem and rubbed her forehead. What do I specially want with them ? Why do I do this ?

But I shall go away for good, replied a clear voice within her, as it seemed. I shall give an hour's notice and be off to-morrow morning at five o'clock. Old Vavrys will take my trunk to the railway. But that will not do, protested Olga puzzled : where should I go from here ? How shall I do without a place ? I shall go home, replied the voice, which had so far settled matters for her. Of course, Mama will cry, but Daddy will approve. It is good so, little daughter, better honour than a good table.

But Daddy, dear, objected Olga with calm and proud joy, what shall I do now ? You will go to the factory, replied the voice which had settled everything : you will do manual labour, take weekly wages and help Mama at home, for she is old and weak. You will wash our linen and scrub the floor : you will go to sleep tired and eat when hungry. Little daughter, you will go home.

Olga threw out her hands in rapture. Hence, hence ! And to-morrow evening I shall be at home. And how was it, indeed, possible that it did not occur to me long ago ? How have I put up with it ? At once, directly after tea I will give notice and go home ; in the evening I shall put everything in order, bring the countess here and show her—this is what I shall take home, if there is a thread of yours pluck it out; only the mud on this dress is yours, my lady, and that I shall take away.

Rosy with joy, Olga flung off her mud-stained dress. To-morrow, to-morrow ! I shall hide myself in the corner of the carriage where no one will even see me : I shall fly like a bird from the cage. She put on a tomboy humour, whistled, and sported a red tie. She smiled at herself in the glass, proudly with tousled hair, and whistled as loudly as she could : C D G D, C D G D.

People rushed about the yard : a hoarse gong sounded for tea. Olga flew downstairs, as she did not want for this last time to miss the spectacle of the imposing entry of the count's family. There, behold, was the old count descending, half-lame, leaning on the shoulder of the haggard Oswald. The countess with her heavy, inflated, sickly body was crossly scolding at Mary and pulling her hair ribbon. Behind lounged athletic Mr. Kennedy, loftily indifferent to all that was going on around him.

The courtly old gentleman reached the door first, opened it and said " Madame."

The countess with heavy steps entered the dining-room.

"Mademoiselle," said the count, glancing at Olga. Olga entered with head erect. After her followed the count, Kennedy, Mary and Oswald. The count seated himself at the head of the table, with the countess on his right and Olga on his left. The countess rang. The maids entered, with eyes cast down and noiseless steps like puppets, who only heard orders and only noticed signs : as though those young lips never uttered a sound and those downcast eyes were never raised in a look indicative of interest, or understanding. Olga with sharp eyes took in the details of this dumb show, "so that I may never forget it again."

"*Du beurre, mademoiselle ?*" asked the count.

"*Merci.*" She drank plain tea with dry bread : in a week, she revelled in the thought, I shall go to the factory. Meanwhile the count laboured with his false teeth, the countess ate nothing, Oswald spilled cocoa on the table-cloth. Mary left everything, but munched sweets, and only Mr. Kennedy spread a centimetre of butter on his slice of bread. Triumphant scorn of everyone and everything filled Olga's heart. Poor folks, to-morrow I shall be the sole one of you who is free. I shall remember those dinners of yours with disgust, when you had nothing to say to each other, no exchange of sympathies, nothing to laugh about.

From a lofty height Olga looked down on Mr. Kennedy. She hated him heartily from the first day : she hated the indifferent facility with which he managed to live his own way, not in the least caring for anyone : she hated him because no one stood up to him and he despised everything and everybody with his detached superiority. Goodness knew why he was there ; he boxed roughly with Oswald, went out with him on horseback, and allowed himself to be idolized by him : he went to shoot when he felt inclined, and when he sprawled somewhere in the park nothing could make him stir. Sometimes when alone he would sit at the piano and make up tunes ; he played perfectly, but without feeling, only thinking of himself ; Olga used to listen secretly, quite offended that she could not enter into this cold, complicated, egotistical music. He paid attention to no one nor anything ; if he were directly asked a question he would scarcely move his lips to say " yes " or " no." A powerful young fellow, ruthless, vain, and lazy, who did everything as with condescension : sometimes the old count ventured to invite him to a game of chess ; then Mr. Kennedy without a word sat down to the chessboard and in a few unconsidered, violent, terribly brutal moves gave check to the old gentleman, who perspired uneasily and stammered like a child, meditating full of excitement half an hour before each move, drawing his piece back fully a dozen times before deciding. Olga regarded this uneven struggle with unconcealed rage; she sometimes used to play chess with the count herself, a good, thoughtful player, when there were endless games full of meditation and considered plans, and to see through them meant flattering the craft of her antagonist and appreciating his play. Olga did not ask if she had a right to it, but felt herself immensely superior to Mr. Kennedy with all his accomplishments, which did not cost him the least effort, and the self-confidence and supreme superiority with which he mastered everyone; she despised him and made him aware of it; yes, all her girlish pride and conceit, outraged so many times daily, revived in this display of contempt.

Meanwhile Mr. Kennedy took his tea with great composure, not in the least minding the hostile glances of Olga glaring. He does not notice, Olga thought excited; and yet every night when he goes to bed he knocks at my door, " Open, Miss Olga."

In fact it was one of the mysteries of the castle, and Olga was not even aware how greatly this mystery interested the servants' hall. The young Englishman, who ignored the chamber-maids in an almost outrageous manner, carried on these secret games a pretty long while. It was his "fancy" that they should arrange a room for him in the castle tower which, it was said for generations, was haunted. Olga did not believe in ghosts at all, and saw in Kennedy's whim only the comedy of a swanker, but this did not prevent her from being in mortal fear on the stairs and in the passage at night. Besides, it is the absolute truth that sounds were heard at night which it was insufficient to refer to Franz's wooings or to other mischief in the women's quarters. In short one night, when Olga already lay down, Mr. Kennedy knocked at her door, "Open, Miss Olga." She then flung a dressing-gown round her and asked through the chink of the door what he wanted. Then Mr. Kennedy began to utter a jumble of nonsense in English of which she scarcely understood a quarter, but just enough to grasp that he called her "sweet Aulga," and other interesting names; this was sufficient for her to slam the door in his face and lock it, and in the morning on first seeing him she asked with severe wide-opened eyes what he was doing at her door at night. Mr. Kennedy did not think it at all necessary to explain or even to make it clear that he remembered anything of it; but from that time he knocked every night, said, "Open, Miss Olga," tried the lock and rattled it in the most waggish manner, while Olga in bed dragged the coverlet up to her chin and screamed tearfully in English : "You're a rascal," or "you are crazy," in all the shades of meaning which that word possesses only in the English language—mortified to despair that this rogue and idiot was laughing. That was his only laugh the whole day long.

Olga gazed with shining eyes at Mr. Kennedy. As soon as he raises his eyes I shall ask him now, before everyone, "Mr. Kennedy, what do you mean by pestering at my room every night ?" There will be a scandal, but before I am leaving I will tell other things. Then Mr. Kennedy looked up with steely-blue, calm eyes : Olga began to move her lips, and suddenly reddened. She remembered——

Those beautiful moonlight nights a week ago were to blame. Inexpressibly enchanting nights, nights of clear full moon in the height of summer, silvery nights, moonlight nights of heathen sanctity. Olga was wandering round the castle, having no mind to go to bed on such an enchanting night ; she was alone and happy, full of winged amazement at the wealth of beauty which flooded the sleeping world. Slowly, with awe, full of delight she ventured into the park. She beheld beauteous birches and deep black oaks in the silvery meadows, mysterious shadows and wondrous light : it was more than one could endure. She went on through a large meadow to the little lake with a fountain ; and when she had gone round the bushes she spied on the edge of the lake the white statue of a man, with face upraised to the full moon, with hands clasped behind the head, with a powerful chest firmly knit above a slender waist. It was Mr. Kennedy. Olga was not a silly girl, did not scream or start to run. With eyes half-closed she gazed fixedly on the white figure. A vigorous movement of the muscles animated the statue. From the calves passed a wave of contracted muscles up to the chest and into the handsome, powerful arms ; again a new muscular wave rose upwards from the slender calves, once more to swell the sculptured biceps of the image. Mr. Kennedy took exercise in this peculiar manner, without stirring from the position. Suddenly he bent backward, lifted his hands, and dived backwards into the lake. The water splashed, glistened, and gurgled. Olga quietly disappeared, and thinking no more of the mysterious and grim shades of night made her way straight home : strange to say, she saw no more the beauteous birches and ancient oaks on silvery lawns. That was the first reason why she blushed.

She really did not know why she should turn

red, especially; there was nothing whatever in the matter to be ashamed of, and there was so much wonderful beauty in that adventure. But something worse happened, and that the very next day. It was a lovely, clear night: Olga took a walk again before the castle, but did not enter the park at all: she thought of Mr. Kennedy, who was perhaps bathing again that day, of the strange deep gloom of the park, of the white statue of the young man; when a gossiping stewardess approached her she avoided her, wishing to be alone. And then it was getting late, eleven o'clock, and Olga was afraid to go home alone along the steps and passages. Kennedy returned from the park, with his hands in his pockets: when he saw Olga he wanted to begin his queer nocturnal courtship, but Olga cut short his speech and commanded him loftily enough to light her home. Kennedy, somewhat puzzled, carried a candle and said nothing: and when they were at her door he said very mildly, " Good night." Olga turned round violently, cast at him a glance unnaturally dark, and without waiting to think at all seized a good handful of his hair. It was moist and gently shaggy, like the hair of a young Newfoundland dog just out of the water. Olga gave a whistle of delight, and without knowing what she was about gave it a hard tug. Before he had come to himself she had slammed the door and locked it. Mr. Kennedy retired as if thunderstruck, but in half an hour he returned, barefooted and apparently half-undressed and knocked gently, whispering " Olga, O Olga ! " She made no reply, and Mr. Kennedy finally stole away.

That incident made Olga now so abashed. It was, of course, shameful stupidity. Olga wanted to sink through the floor for what she had done, but at least she paid out Mr. Kennedy in double measure, for he was to blame for it. The next night she took the rough-coated pug Fritz into her room ; when Kennedy came to knock Fritz set up a terrific howling. For a few days Mr. Kennedy kept quiet, but twice he had come round again and chattered in a most lyrical manner, whereupon Olga, sick of it and full of violent hatred of this impudent fellow, buried her ears in the pillow so as not to hear.

That was, I vow, all that had passed between Olga and Mr. Kennedy : and on this account she was so unutterably miserable that she reddened at his glance, and could have struck herself for it. She was vexed beyond measure in her touchy maidenly heart. So much the better, she said to herself, that I go : if for no other reason than on account of that man. She felt weary of the daily struggle and humbled by her own feebleness ; such a torrent of disgust and resentment rose in her throat that she could have cried out. Glory be to Thee, Lord, she forced herself into ease, that I am going: if I stopped a day longer I should set up a most fearful scandal.

"*Prenez des prunes, mademoiselle.*"

"*Pardon, madame?*"

"*Prenez des prunes.*"

"*Merci, merci, madame la comtesse.*"

She turned her thoughts away from Mr. Kennedy and her glance fell upon the handsome face of Oswald. Her heart was slightly cheered by a feeling of kindly tenderness. It was no secret from her that the boy was in love with her in his own way; he was, of course, unable to confess it except by unnecessary rudeness and averted eyes. On the other hand Olga took special delight in tormenting him; she would put her hand round his pretty, delicate neck and drag him along the park, enjoying immensely his growling and blissful rage. There, just then, aware of her glance, he swallowed an immense mouthful and glared savagely. Poor Oswald! What will become of you, in that dreadful house, child about to become a youth, weighed down at the same time by an excess of delicacy and ferocity? How will your heart open, and what examples will you see? A spasm of ill-temper struck Olga. Not long ago she had gone into Oswald's room and caught him pounding and boxing the chambermaid Paulina, the worst of all the girls. Ah, one understood, it was only the play of a noisy puppy ; but Oswald had no business to flare up, Pauline had no need to have eyes and face so inflamed, in short that should never have happened, certainly, certainly. Olga, full of suspicion, put herself from that time on guard : she never again passed sensitive fingers through Oswald's hair, never placed her hand on his neck, but began to regard him with Argus eyes, full of alarm and stooping even to spying —resolved not to expose Oswald's childhood to premature and shameful temptation. Often she suddenly ran away from Mary to look after Oswald ; she was coldly severe with him, but only achieved that his youthful love was penetrated with rebellious hatred. But why, Olga now asked herself, should I specially look after him ? What have I, an outsider, to do with whatever lessons on life Paulina or any other creature gives him ? Why should I plague myself with uneasiness and my own severity, which hurts ¦me more than him ? Good-bye, good-bye, Oswald, I shall not tell you that you are my dear child, I shall not tell you that I have loved your boyish innocence, more lovable than girlish innocence ; I shall not look after you, just open your eyes and both arms to seize the first opportunity—I shall not be there to weep over you.

And you, my lady, Olga suddenly entered upon another reckoning, you have suspected me. You have spied on the time I have passed with Oswald; you have made it evident to me that "it is better for him to be in the company of Mr. Kennedy." Perhaps it is also better for him to be in the company of Paulina. Paulina is your confidante. When one night Oswald went out with Kennedy secretly to catch an otter you came into my room, I had to let you in; you sought the boy even under the coverlet of my bed. Very well, my lady, he is your child: but you send Paulina to his bedroom to awaken him, Paulina, a woman over thirty and as perverted as a demon. You search my wardrobe and sniff about my chest of drawers; then you call me into your carriage in order to entertain you. You offer me prunes, thank you, Madame, you are so kind. If you set me down for frivolous and for a thief, do send me from the table to go to the servants' hall, or rather to the laundry; there I shall swallow a bit of bread with tears of rage and humiliation, but at least, at least I shall not be obliged to smile.

"Don't you hear, miss?"

"Pardon," Olga reddened.

"Perhaps you are—a little—unwell," asked

the count gazing keenly at her. " Are you not, perhaps—feverish ? "

" No, my lord," objected Olga hastily. " There is nothing whatever the matter with me."

" So much the better," uttered the count slowly. " I don't care for—invalids ! "

Olga's spirits fell at once. I am not a match for these people, she felt despairingly, I do not know how to stand against them. God, give me strength to give notice to-day ! God, give me that strength ! She was dreadfully afraid of telling the count. He would certainly raise his eyebrows and say : " At once, miss ? Such a thing is not done."

If I could only contrive ! How can I explain that I must, must go home immediately, on the instant ? I shall run away if I am not allowed to go, I shall certainly run away ! Tearfully Olga awaited the moments to come.

The family rose from the tea-table and settled down in the next room ; the count and Kennedy smoked, the countess snatched up some embroidery ; the afternoon post was expected. As soon as the children go out, decided Olga, I will speak about it. In the meantime with beating heart she forced herself to think of her home. She pictured her mother in a blue apron, the plain deal furniture all scrubbed, her father without his coat smoking as he read the newspaper with thoughtful solicitude. That is my only refuge, she felt with growing anxiety, I shall not bear this another day. O Lord, grant me strength in the last moment!

Paulina with downcast eyes brought the letters on a silver salver. The count collected the letters on his lap: he wanted to take also the last letter set aside, but Paulina respectfully withdrew her hand.

"For mademoiselle," she murmured.

Ah, from a distance Olga recognized her mother's letter, the pitiful, stained envelope directed in a shocking spelling, a letter of which she was always ashamed and yet which she carried next to her heart. She blushed also to-day—forgive me, Mamma! With trembling fingers she took the dear little country letter, and with emotion read through the too elaborately written address as though the world were evil and refused to yield a letter without detailed direction to the right hands so far away, among strange people—but at that moment a weight fell from her heart: Mamma, how you have helped me! I will read the letter and suddenly cry out that my father is ill, I must go to him, I will get my things and be off, and no one will be able to detain me : in a week I will write that I must stay at home, and let them send my trunk after me. That will be the easiest plan. She joyfully said to herself.

As with every woman, it was clearly easier to help herself by means of excuses than through giving reasons. Full of delight she tore open the envelope. When she drew out the letter she felt a sudden pang, held her breath and began to read :

Dear little Daughter,

i must rite you the sad news that yer Dad is il doctor sed it is 'is 'eart and that he is week and 'is feet have swelled and he can't walk doctor ses he mustn't be exited about anything doctor ses you mustn't complane when you are writing to us Dad wurris and frets about it don't do it but write that you are very well so that he won't be upset You know how fond he is of you and that you are in a good place Heaven be thanked.

Pray for Dad and do not come it is no end of a jurny of the World we have received the muny thank you many times it is very bad for us that Dad is laid up Franky has stolen his watch we can't tel him about it it would kil him we have said it is at the watchmaker's. All the time he keeps on asking when it will be mended as he can't tell the time and I can't cry before him.

Dear daughter I must write you to thank God you have such a nice place Pray for your master and mistress and serve them faithfully there's no such good place if you eat all the good grub there itl do you good you are week in the chest and send us something ebery month daughter and we thank you God will reward you for yer fambly.

Remember what a master you've got. If you will serve them many years they will look after you til deth it's as good as guvment don't get yerself talkt about Dad is waistin dayly.

My respex to the mistress.

Your loving mother,
Kostelec no 37.

The count ceased reading his letters and stared at Olga.

"Mademoiselle, you are unwell," he exclaimed in actual terror.

Olga rose listlessly and pressed her hands to her temples.

" Just—my head, my lord," she gasped.

" Go and lie down at once, miss, go and lie down at once," cried the count peremptorily and disquieted.

Olga bowed mechanically and slowly went out.

The count cast a questioning glance at his wife; she shrugged her shoulders and said sharply : " *Oswald, gerade sitzen.*"

Mr. Kennedy smoked and gazed at the ceiling. There was disconcerting silence.

The countess went on sewing with contracted lips. After a while she rang and Pauline appeared.

" Paulina, where has mademoiselle gone ? " she asked, scarcely opening her mouth.

187

" To her room, my lady," replied the maid, " and has locked herself in."

" Have the horses ready."

The carriage wheels rattled on the sand in the yard, and the coachman led the horses and buckled straps.

" *Papa, soll ich reiten?* " ventured Oswald.

" *Ja,* " nodded the count, with a blank stare.

The countess turned on him a searching and hostile glance.

" *Wirst du mitfahren?* " she asked.

" *Nein,* " he said absently.

The groom brought the riding horses and saddled them. Kennedy's horse danced all round the yard before allowing himself to be saddled, while Oswald's half-blooded animal peacefully and wisely pawed the ground, sadly contemplating his own hoof.

The family went out to the courtyard. Oswald, a good horseman, at once vaulted on his horse into the saddle and could not refrain from casting a glance up at Olga's window as she so often waved her hand to him when he was starting for his ride. There was nobody at the window.

The countess heavily climbed into the carriage.

" Mary," she called back peremptorily.

Little Mary made a face but followed her

into the carriage. The countess was not yet quite ready.

"Paulina," she called the chambermaid, "go, see what Miss Olga is doing. But don't let her catch you."

Mr. Kennedy threw away his cigarette, with one bound he was in the saddle and pressed his knees. The horse sprang forward galloping through the vaulted entrance, striking echo in thunder from the boarded floor of the subway, lightning sparks from the cobbled pavement before the castle.

"Hullo, Mr. Kennedy," shouted Oswald boyishly and dashed after him.

Paulina came running back, her hands in the pockets of her white apron.

"Madam," she reported confidentially, "Miss Olga is hanging up her dresses in her wardrobe and is arranging her linen in her chest of drawers."

The countess waved her hand. "Go on," she called to the coachmen.

The carriage moved off, the old count waved a greeting and he was alone. He sat down on the bench under the arcade, his stick between his knees and bad-humouredly and forlornly he stared out into the courtyard. For half an hour he sat there; and then he stood up and heavily clumped with his paralysed limbs into the drawing-room. He sat down in the arm-chair beside the chessboard where the game which he had been playing yesterday with Olga was still unfinished. He scrutinized the board, obviously he was in a tight corner ; Olga had brought up her knight and was attacking. He bent over the chessboard in the effort to foresee her moves : then her neat little scheme which made his own defeat certain dawned upon him. Then he stood up, and erect, went upstairs with clattering stick to the guest quarters. He halted before Olga's door. It was quiet, quite alarmingly quiet, nothing stirred. At length he knocked, "Miss Olga, how are you ? "

A moment's silence.

"Better now, thank you," said Olga in a constrained voice. "Do you want anything, my lord ? "

"No, no, just lie down." And suddenly as if he thought that he had said too much and that he might spoil it, he added : "So that you will be able to teach to-morrow." Then he noisily descended to the drawing-room.

If he had remained a little longer he would have heard feeble groans, broken by ceaseless silent weeping.

Lonely hours are long, very long. At length the carriage returned, the heated horses were being led up and down the yard, and from the kitchen began the usual flustered rattle, as on every day. At half-past seven the gong rang for supper. All were seated, but Olga was missing. For a moment all went on as if not noticing this, until the old count raised his eyebrows and asked in surprise, "*Was, die Olga kommt nicht?*"

The countess shot a glance at him and was silent. Not until after a pretty long time she called to Paulina: "Ask Miss Olga what she wants to eat."

Paulina was back in an instant.

"My lady, Miss Olga desires to thank you but she is not hungry and will get up tomorrow."

The countess slightly tossed her head; there was more than dissatisfaction in that.

Oswald merely trifled with his food and cast beseeching glances at Mr. Kennedy as if imploring him to take him off outside as soon as possible when the meal was over: but Mr. Kennedy, as usual, did not choose to understand.

By now twilight had come, bringing the evening so merciful for those who are tired, so endlessly tedious for those unhappy. There is light, it darkens and night is here; one cannot tell when exactly this darkness starts which stifles and oppresses one, darkness, that abyss of darkness in the depth of which human despair wallows. You silent night, you know, you who hear the breathing of those asleep and the groans of the sick, for you have listened carefully to hear the feeble, feverish breath of a girl who has wept long and now no longer weeps ; you have held your ear to her heart and heavily contracted throat enwrapped in tousled hair. You have heard sobs smothered in the pillow and then the silence that was even more terrible.

You have heard, dumb night, how the silence has spread over floor by floor, room by room, and you who with burning fingers stifled a woman's cry of love in the corner of the staircase. You lent echo to the steps of a young man, with hair still wet after bathing, as he strolled belated to his bed gently whistling along the lengthy castle passage.

Dark night, you have seen how a young girl, worn with weeping, trembled at the sound of those young steps. You saw how she bounded off the bed as if hurled forward by some blind force, threw back her hair from her burning forehead, dashing to the door, unlocked it and left it ajar. Then once more she lay rigid on her feverish bed in terrible expectation, as one for whom there is no help.